RED WIZARD

Atheneum Books by Nancy Springer

Not on a White Horse
They're All Named Wildfire
Red Wizard

RED WIZARD

Nancy Springer

Atheneum · 1990 · New York

For Jonathan, a little bit late

Atheneum
Macmillan Publishing Company
866 Third Avenue, New York, NY 10022
Collier Macmillan Canada, Inc.
First Edition
Printed in the United States of America
10 9 8 7 6 5 4 3 2 1
Designed by Nancy Williams

Library of Congress Cataloging-in-Publication Data
Springer, Nancy.
Red Wizard / Nancy Springer.—1st ed.
p. cm.
Summary: Seventh-grader Ryan is whisked from his world into a fantasy kingdom by an incompetent wizard trying to find the perfect color red, but the mistake may avert a crisis with a rebel warlock and help Ryan solve a problem with his own father.
ISBN 0–689–31485–X
[1. Fathers and sons–Fiction. 2. Fantasy.] I. Title.
PZ7.S76846Re 1990
[Fic]–dc19 88–29376 CIP AC

RED WIZARD

Chapter 1

Sinoper, minium, cinnabar, kermes," the little man muttered, counting off on his pudgy fingers, "madder, murrey, lac—good reds all, orange reds and purple reds, rose reds and dark reds, but there's not a true, pure, oxblood red among them."

He lived alone, far from the other wizards, near a deposit of the alum he needed for his dyes. Being lonely, he often talked to himself and answered himself as well.

At various times he had tried out many pigments on the oak-slab cottage walls around him, until every visible bit of the wood wore a motley of colors, some already fading, others shouting and clashing with each other for attention. Just as variously colored, strips of cloth hung fluttering from the rafters overhead; his experiments. And lately he had started laying colors on the floor, those portions of it he could reach through the clutter of clay pots and porringers and piled dyestuffs. The muddle of colors all around him matched the muddle in his mind.

"Sinoper is dull," he complained to the tatterdemalion cottage or the world, "minium is poisonous, kermes is more purple than red, the rest of them are fugitives all. I ought to do a proper magic for a true, pure, steadfast red. And I will, if the sun is in Mars—or is it Jupiter, for red?" He plunged his arms into the mess on his plank table without finding anything to help him, ran a splinter into his finger, and swore mildly. "Stars and garters! I can never remember. Mars, I think, and the dark of the moon, for iron, but what is the symbol? Where is that blasted folio?"

There could have been a warthog hidden in his cottage, and he would not have been likely to find it. He did not immediately locate his leather-bound guide to the magical symbols and correspondences.

"Hang it all!" he exploded after a brief search. "I'll do it my own way, and a pox on the rubrics."

The bench by the table stood stacked with dirty brown madder roots. He tumbled them onto the floor to clear a seat for his body, for he knew he would forget all about the plump thing while he was working. He sat, and then his bayberry gray eyes grew round and still as he concentrated.

"Red," he murmured. "Ruddy, ruddle, Rudd, Ryan, red."

He blinked and wondered briefly who or what were Rudd and Ryan. Then he discounted the question and let himself drift deeper into his trance, his magical quest for a loyal and sanguine red.

"B-b-b-b-b-b-blooey," Ryan babbled his lips at the muttering ocean. It slopped back without answering. Just like parents. Couldn't talk with them. And their idea of a vacation was like a bad dream. Somehow they had found this offshore island with no cars, no road to run them on, nothing but sand dunes. No TV, no movies, no library. Nothing but a dozen phlegmatic islanders and a general store, the warm Carolina sunshine and the melancholy gulls. No matter how many times Ryan walked around the island, he couldn't see anything more. Shore and seawater lay bleached white with glare, faded as his old jeans. Colorless.

Magic Island, they called this place. Huh. To Ryan, magic meant wizards and warlocks, fierce eyes, fingers crackling fire, excitement. But this island was about as exciting as oatmeal.

He turned back to the rented bungalow. On the screened-in porch with its ocean view, his parents sat sipping decaffeinated iced tea and diddling at an enormous jigsaw puzzle. Why anyone would want to do a jigsaw puzzle of a bowl of vegetables, Ryan could not fathom. He watched his mother fit an eye onto a potato and felt hopeless. "Bored" did not entirely describe what was wrong. He was worn out with not rocking the boat, not making waves. He felt like old bones mumbled bare by the ocean and spat up on the beach, sucked dry and bleached white as the sand. But he knew that his parents, like his teachers, had had their fill of his crazy thoughts, his leaps of mind. He said what other kids would say.

"Mom," he complained, "there's nothing to do."

Emily DeWitt focused her soft blue eyes, the color of a washed-out sky, on her son. She tried to glare. She did not glare very well and resorted to words. "Ryan," she warned. The family vacation was intended as a medical treatment for Ryan's father, to relax him and relieve his stress-related symptoms. Ryan was under orders not to annoy him.

"I can't help it," he said, keeping his eyes on his mother. He had been on the island with his parents for a week and had passed the time mostly in daydreaming, wearing all his favorite fantasies threadbare. Even daydreaming has its limits.

"Go buy yourself a book at the store," she suggested.

"There's nothing good there. I looked."

In fact he had looked and looked. There were a few battered paperbacks, mostly bad westerns. Nope, the storekeeper had said, he didn't expect any more books. Last week's newspapers would come over on the boat next week. Some magazines would come in next month for the summer people. Ryan's folks were the earliest of the lot. Too bad, sonny.

Ryan said to his mother, "If there were just some comic books, even. . . ."

Mr. DeWitt roused, snorting like an old war-horse hearing a distant bugle call. "It's a blessing there aren't," he rumbled. "I've said it time and again, you read far too much. A boy your age ought to be out playing ball—"

"Henry," interrupted Mrs. DeWitt, "now hush. You'll get your blood pressure up."

"Don't hush me, Emily! You know I wouldn't mind if it was doing him any good, but it's not." Ryan's father glared at him. He knew how to glare like an expert, and Ryan felt his own gaze growing vague and lumpish to avoid giving in to the glare. He knew he could not win with adults, so he had learned to appear not to care. When he was off in his own world, nothing could touch him. He hardly even saw what was around him.

"I swear his mind's turning to mush!" Mr. DeWitt burst out.

Ryan stood staring hazily at the pine-plank floor, and his father barked at him.

"You want something to do, go study your geometry!"

Mr. DeWitt was a successful businessman with his own small company, and he badly wanted his son to be an even greater success, someone to build "DeWitt Office Supplies" into "DeWitt Enterprises," a name and a power in the business world. But Ryan had not gotten a single good mark in seventh grade, not even in language arts. He had tried, but his brain seemed to make connections differently from other people's. In elementary school his teachers had said he was creative, but in junior high they just said he was giving the wrong answers. He had tried for the first few months, but after Christmas he had spent the year day-dreaming, forgetting his assignments, and reading all the fantasy adventure novels he could get his hands on. It was no use trying to talk with his teachers, any more than it was with his parents.

"Henry," said Mrs. DeWitt in a firmer tone, "stop shouting. Ryan." She fixed her son with her mild cerulean gaze. "Remember our agreement."

There had been a choice. Ryan was either to go with his parents to the island off the shore of North Carolina and be cheerful about it, or stay with his aunt and attend summer school. He had chosen Magic Island.

Ryan focused on his mother. "I didn't know it was going to be like this," he complained.

"Ryan!" Mr. DeWitt thundered at him. "Stop whining!"

Dull, colorless, everything around him, even his own dreams. . . . Ryan found he had retreated as far as he could for the time and had to turn. For the first time since he had entered the bungalow he looked straight at his father. "You hate me," he said.

Mr. DeWitt sputtered. Before his father could collect himself and answer, Ryan slammed out of the bungalow and disappeared.

Really disappeared.

The constable's report stated that he was last seen heading toward the general store, wearing T-shirt, torn jeans, and old jogging shoes. The storekeeper said that yep, the boy had been in. Bought something. A packet of crayons with one missing had been found lying in the sandy street outside the store. Yep, the storekeeper decided, he reckoned the boy had bought the crayons. Nope, he hadn't seen which way the kid went.

After Ryan failed to appear for supper, the DeWitts and the island constable searched all night. The next day the state police were called in.

"But where could he *be*?" Mr. DeWitt pleaded when the officers came to give their report. "You say there are no boats missing, nobody took him over to the mainland, he's not in anybody's house or any of the empty summer houses."

"We searched every building on this island ground to attic," said the constable. "We even looked in refrigerators. The old dug wells are all filled in. We checked the cisterns. We checked the church steeple. Can't nobody think of noplace else he could be."

"He must have been kidnapped," whispered Mrs. DeWitt.

"If he was, you would have got a ransom demand," said the state trooper.

"What if somebody took him for—for—"

"No weirdos on this island," said the constable firmly. "Ain't nobody strange been around and can't nothing much happen here without everybody knowing. Can't nobody get on or off the island without everybody knowing, neither. No, ma'am, I think there's only one explanation."

The DeWitts stood with their arms around each other, staring at the man who was about to break their hearts.

"I think the boy must have drowned somehow," the constable said. "Body might never be recovered."

Mr. DeWitt stiffened angrily, then shouted, "Why would he drown? He's not a three-year-old. He knows how to swim!"

"Undertow," the constable said. "Or maybe . . ." He let his voice trail away.

Cued, the state trooper spoke. "You say he was despondent when he left. Suicide's a big problem with juveniles these days. I'm sorry, Mr. DeWitt. I'm sorry, ma'am."

Mr. DeWitt's face went brick red. He lunged at the trooper to hit him. "Henry!" Mrs. DeWitt screamed, grabbing him by the arm, and the officer stepped back.

"I'll go," he said. "I know you're upset." He left the cottage.

"It's the only logical explanation," the constable added awkwardly before he followed. "Sorry, ma'am. Sorry, sir."

Both police officers walked off into the dusk.

At first, that long night, Emily and Henry DeWitt could not bear to look at each other. Later, they clung together and cried. On toward dawn they reached the odd, taut calm that people sometimes find, faced with the most terrible things that could happen to them. The DeWitts were living their worst nightmare. Ryan was their only child.

Sometime after sunrise Ryan's father spoke. "I'm not ready to give up, Emily. Don't plan the funeral yet. You think I'm crazy?"

She shook her head. Her husband tightened his arm around her.

"I don't care what they say. He'd not dead."

"I feel that way, too," whispered Ryan's mother. "He just can't be killed. We'd know it if he was."

Think, Mr. DeWitt commanded himself. Think where Ryan could have gone. He wished he knew the boy better. He worried: If he and Ryan had been closer, if Ryan had never said, "You hate me," might this somehow not have happened? He toughened his mind against that feeling. No use thinking what might have been. No use thinking about the past. Think what was to be done now. Where might Ryan be?

"No other logical explanation," he grumbled. "Huh. There must be an illogical explanation, then."

He was quite correct. Though it was to be some time before he started to understand the ways of wizardry.

Chapter 2

Ryan appeared out of air in front of the startled wizard: a moderately attractive boy dressed in uncouth shoes, a pair of coarse indigo trousers with orange stitching, and a peculiar, soft-textured shirt with I ♥ NEW YORK printed across the front. He stood clutching something tightly in one gangling hand. His eyes bugged, and his mouth moved several times before he managed to exlaim, "What the heck is going on! I was just coming out of the store—"

"Aloysius Persyvaunce, master wizard, at your service," gasped that portly gentleman, equally shaken. "May I ask your name?"

"Ryan DeWitt." He stood running his eyes wildly around the low-roofed, riotously particolored, jumbled building in which he stood. Against the carnival-hued walls stood plank shelves, daubed just as bright, piled high with strange objects: greasy blue-green and powdery yellow rocks, chunks of wood, lichens, dead branches crusted thick with dead bugs. On the table, topping a heap of nameless debris, lay a slither of what appeared to be—squid? Octopus? Something with tentacles, anyway. Ryan took a hasty step back from the gut-gray things. "Is this some sort of joke?" he demanded.

Persyvaunce came out of his stupor of astonishment and bustled to pull out an elk's-horn chair for the boy, brushing rolls of cherry bark off it onto the floor. "No, no, not at all," he exclaimed. "Please be seated. No joke, no joke at all." He perched on his bench opposite Ryan: a small, plump man, his legs so short that his slippered toes barely touched the floor. "I am dreadfully sorry," he said earnestly. "It seems—I believe—I am very much afraid I have summoned you out of your own world somehow."

"Last I knew, I was in North Carolina," Ryan protested, "and there's never been *anything* like this there!"

Persyvaunce groaned and put his head in his hands. His hair grew in wisps, Ryan noticed, and the pink skin of his scalp showed through, like a baby's. "Just as I feared," the wizard lamented into his hands. "A place I've never heard of. When, oh, when will I ever learn. . . . It's an island, I suppose?"

Too shaken to expand on the geography of North Carolina, Ryan merely nodded.

Persyvaunce said, "Islands are especially susceptible to our magic. England is an island, you know." He meant to explain how Ryan had reached England as it had never been, a magical England. But Ryan scarcely heard. Something Persyvaunce had said was just starting to sink in.

"You're a—a wizard?"

"A master wizard, yes."

He looked not at all like a wizard, Ryan thought. Though Persyvaunce was a grown man, he stood no taller than Ryan himself. Round-faced, round-shouldered, round-bellied, the little sorcerer looked soft all over, like a dumpling. He wore a tunic and some sort of leg wrapping, both thread worn but brightly dyed; the effect was clownish. A tattered, splattered yellow tunic, rust red leggings, and a rotund stranger inside them, that was all Ryan saw of this wizard. No flowing robe, no mystic symbols embroidered in thread of gold. No flying beard and fiery eyes.

"I am a certified specialist in colors," Persyvaunce declared. His round face, as pink as his scalp, glowed with modest pride, but then his expression turned glum. "I was just sort of feeling about for a nice red, a faithful, agreeable, robust, succulent sort of red, if you understand what I mean, and I got you." Persyvaunce eyed him vaguely, as if trying to recognize him. "Do you know someone named Rudd, by chance?"

Ryan blinked. "No."

"Are you particularly fond of red?"

"I—I . . ."

Persyvaunce nodded, sympathetic already.

"I was so bored," Ryan explained, or tried to explain. "Or sort of, like, empty. So I went to the store to get these crayons. That's all they had, crayons. No markers, no poster paper. But I knew we had some scrap paper at the bungalow."

"I see," Persyvaunce murmured. Actually he had never heard of paper, markers, or crayons, and he was struggling very hard to follow. "I don't understand," he admitted on second thought, "about the crayons."

"They're for little kids to color with." Hastily Ryan added, "I haven't touched any in years. It was just because I was so bored."

Still bewildered, Persyvaunce nodded.

"All they had was the small box," Ryan said. "Eight colors. But you wouldn't believe how glad I was to get them. I opened the box as soon as I was out the door."

"And of course you took the red one first," said Persyvaunce, beginning to understand.

"Yeah. I did."

"And I was saying a spell for red," the wizard continued with growing excitement, "hoping for some sort of nibble, you know—and I believe I said a strange word that just came to me, not 'crayon' exactly but something like it. Krae-oh-lah . . ."

Ryan said, "Crayola. Sure. I've got one here."

He extended his hand, opened it, and the round little wizard gasped as if his heart had stopped. In the boy's grubby palm lay a rod of pure, shimmering color, a creamy, shining essence of cramoisie hue. Even the wrapping that encased it glowed with a muted, velvety perfection, softly embracing the deeper, jewellike sheen of the tip.

"That—that is for children?" Persyvaunce cried, choking on the words.

"Sure, to color with. Look." Ryan scraped the crayon over the stained and mottled surface of the bench, leaving a trail of scarlet.

"Oh, don't scratch it!" Persyvaunce yelped, springing up. "Lord, men spend their lives searching for such a red! Blood will serve, but blood doesn't dry true. Maybe if kings had such things as—as crayons, they would make less war. There is a jewel nearly like that, but jewels are hard, cold, and grind down to nothing but white powder, and that is—"

"Nothing but wax." Ryan blinked at the ardent little man. "Heck, in a decent store I could get you a box of sixty-four different colors."

"Oh!" Persyvaunce moaned, sinking back to his seat. "Oh! I can't stand it!"

"Are you all right?"

"Fine, fine." Persyvaunce smiled feebly at him. "Your world is very blessed, to possess such—ah—playthings. For children."

"Yeah. I guess." A dark tone crept into Ryan's voice; he was thinking of his world, with its constant threat of nuclear destruction, of his parents, his school—he hadn't made out very well in the fierce seventh-grade popularity wars. But mostly, his parents. They would wonder where he was, and it served them right.

"Mr. Persyvaunce," he asked abruptly, "can I stay here awhile? Like, maybe overnight. I'd like to see you do some magic."

"My dear boy, of course you're welcome to stay as long as you like!" Persyvaunce popped up from his seat in consternation. "The problem is going to be getting you back at all, ever. I haven't the faintest notion how to go about it!"

"What?" Ryan goggled at the wizard. "Can't you just send me back the way you brought me?"

"I've never sent anything back, my dear friend! Never had any need to." The wizard's mouth as he spoke opened soft and round with dismay. "Anyway, I don't really know how I got you. You seem to have come with that red, er, crayon of yours. You must have been—um—attached to it. And I don't really know how I got the crayon, either. Oh, dear, I am such a poor excuse for a sorcerer." Persyvaunce looked as if he might cry. The sight of the fat little wizard's trembling lower lip made Ryan feel an odd ache, a longing, for what he scarcely knew. "Here you are, quite thoroughly misplaced, and your mother and father will be frantic, and it's all my fault. . . . Oh, dear."

"It's all right," said Ryan. "My parents won't care."

The wizard's eyes widened. "Dear me," said Persyvaunce.

"They won't. Really. They hate me."

Anger underlay the flat words, making Ryan appear sullen, though under the anger, again, lay something more. Persyvaunce looked, and the trembling of his lip stopped, and his moist eyes grew quiet and thoughtful. But he said only, "My colleagues will do their best to find you a way home. I must send messages at once. Help me clear the table a bit, lad."

Ryan stood up but stopped short of touching the limp, squidlike things atop the heap. Persyvaunce, however, forthrightly scooped them up, putting yet more stains on his yellow tunic.

"Cuttlefish," he explained. "I make sepia out of their ink

sacs. I was considering eating the rest, but the thought of having them for supper makes my gorge rise. To the midden heap they go." The wizard headed out the door, with tentacles dangling down from his arms.

He was gone a good while. By the time he returned, with three brown eggs in one plump hand, Ryan had managed to clear a modest portion of the table down to the surface, setting aside flasks and mussel shells, bits of cloth, nameless pebbles and leaves, dirty crockery with mold growing on it. . . . He found the wood, as he might have expected, particolored with pigment spills, nearly as circus bright as the walls.

"Have you seen my slab and muller?" Persyvaunce asked, setting down the eggs.

"Your what?"

The items in question turned out to be a smooth rectangle of marble and a marble round, for grinding. Persyvaunce climbed on a bench to reach a high shelf and returned with a glass flask full of yellow powder. He tied a kerchief around his mouth and nose before he tipped a small amount of the pigment out on the slab.

"Stand back," he told Ryan. "Orpiment is a deadly poison."

Ryan jerked back and watched with rigid attention as Persyvaunce sprinkled a few drops of water onto the orpiment powder from the bucket dipper, then ground pigment and water together into a damp paste.

"It's only poisonous if you swallow a bit," Persyvaunce remarked as he labored, his voice muffled by the kerchief.

"Lead is worse. If you so much as breathe the dust or the vapors, over the course of time you will sicken and die."

"You work with this stuff?" Ryan demanded.

"Yes. The pit and vat and oven are out near the midden. In the open air, the danger is less."

"But—why? Just for a little paint?"

The wizard glanced at him in muted surprise. "Nothing gives a more candid and amiable white than lead," he said, "and it gives a pleasant scarlet, orange, and yellow as well." As if he had never questioned that fine pigments, colors, were worth risking life for.

Ryan said, "Why don't you just, you know, use magic instead of grinding it?"

Persyvaunce sighed. "For some things magic is good," he said, "but for most things, alas, hard work is far better."

He ground until he was certain that every speck of the orpiment was moistened and bound into its paste. Then with a wooden spatula he scraped the paste into a large clamshell.

"Orpiment, now, is a bad character," he admitted. "I would love to find a golden yellow to replace orpiment. It wars with verdigris, it will not let any color lie fair on it, and it attacks parchment. But at least it does not fade. Now, to temper it."

Persyvaunce had taken off his kerchief and washed his hands in the water bucket as he talked. He dried them on the back of his tunic, chose an egg, cracked it, and let the white drip into a pottery bowl. The yolk he kept back, tipping it out of the shell into the palm of one hand.

"What the—" Ryan gave up trying to talk and watched, openmouthed, as the wizard rolled the egg yolk from one hand to the other and back again, pulling long globs of the clinging white away from it with deft fingers, patting at it with his kerchief, all without breaking it. When he was done, he threw the kerchief in a corner, and the egg yolk lay dry in its silky membrane, nestled like a plump cinnabar sun in the hollow of the wizard's palm.

"Yowsers," Ryan breathed. "Is that magic?"

"Not at all."

"But I can't even flip a fried egg without breaking the yolk."

"Luckily this egg must have been in the nest a few days. They don't handle as well when they're quite fresh." Persyvaunce picked up the dried-off egg yolk by a pinch of its membrane between two fingers, so that it hung heavily, bloated with itself.

"Ish," said Ryan.

"Neither white nor membrane must go in the tempera, you see," said Persyvaunce, and with the tip of a knife he slit the pendulous egg yolk so that its rich innards spilled onto the orpiment. He dropped the emptied membrane on the floor, took his wooden spatula, and used its handle to mix his paint.

"Wonderful," he breathed as the orpiment blended with its egg binder. "There is nothing like egg tempera for a fat, fruity, lustrous yellow, or blue, or red—"

"Doesn't it make everything look yellow?"

"Not at all, lad, not at all. Now for parchment."

He brought out what had once quite plainly, by its shape, been an animal skin, though it was translucent and papery and stiff.

"Vellum," Persyvaunce explained in answer to Ryan's glance. "Calfskin. The very best," he expanded. "See how white?"

He scraped clear more of the cluttered table, laid the vellum down, rubbed it all over with pumice, and cut it into careful squares with his knife.

Then the wizard found himself a rather bedraggled brush, sat down, and started painting a curious circular design on one of the vellum squares. It took Ryan a few moments to realize that this was Persyvaunce's message to a fellow wizard. Half the afternoon had gone to get paint and parchment ready, and Ryan had nearly forgotten what they were for.

"I wouldn't want to alarm them too much," Persyvaunce said without looking up, "so I'm using yellow, not red. The tortoise is my device, and everyone knows it."

Inside the circle was an oval with hexagonal scales and elongated daubs by way of head, tail, and feet. Ryan could see that it was meant to be a turtle, sort of. Persyvaunce went on to the next vellum square.

"We each have a device," he added after he had finished all the squares, as if he had just spoken, though half an hour had gone by in silence. "Come out into the garden, and we will send them off." The wizard headed out the door with vellums in hand, and Ryan followed.

Wild and overgrown and riotous with color, the garden rambled among immense, ancient oaks and rosebushes as tall as fruit trees. Chickens, charcoal black or golden brown with white speckles, roamed and clucked everywhere. Pea vines and runner beans in blossom frothed along strings stretched between oaks and elms and beeches. Intensely yellow celandine, blue larkspur and cornflower and forget-me-not, purple pansies, and pink foxglove jostled with vegetables for growing space. Bees buzzed around the flowers, then zoomed to basket hives set along a hedge. Farther along hulked the midden, then the pit where Persyvaunce's lead coils lay corroding white in the fumes of vinegar and the heat of dung, and then the stand and crossbar supporting the huge kettle he used to boil woad. Midden, pit, and kettle each gave off a pungent odor that eddied amid the fragrance of all the flowers. Ryan shied away from pit and midden, walked to the opposite hedge, and looked through; beyond lay forest, the most tangled and forbidding of forest. To either side loomed bare, blunt mountains, locker-room gray. Ryan felt a chill in the air despite the sunshine. Not much like North Carolina, this place.

"Here we are," the wizard remarked, and he laid the vellums on a neglected birdbath made of a real tortoise's shell. Persyvaunce stood back, closed his eyes, and took a deep breath. Slowly he let it out. The vellums, though nothing touched them, stirred, turned diamondwise. Each fluttered two diagonal corners as if gathering strength or nerve, then rose and swooped away. They all sailed off in different directions, looking at first like topaz-patterned butterflies, then more like kites with no strings to hold them down.

"There," said Persyvaunce. He stood eyeing the sky absently for several moments after the vellums were gone from sight. "Silver blue," he murmured. "If a blue could indeed be made from silver, it would look like that." Then he seemed to feel Ryan's gaze on him, gave a little jump, and turned. "Sorry," he remarked. "Are you hungry?"

Ryan nodded but asked, "How did you make the vellums fly?"

"Ah, lad, you'll have to go to the college if you wish to be a wizard. Dinner. I must make dinner." The little wizard hurried into the cottage.

Ryan stayed outside, looking around, shivering in the evening chill, though more from excitement and strain than from cold. Magic! Everywhere around him, in the closing, rose-colored bean flowers, in the silvery sky going dusky gray—he could feel the magic, almost touch it, and the sense of its presence thrilled him. It nearly filled him, nearly sent away the empty, hollow feeling that had been bothering him lately. Nearly.

When the sky turned from dusky to dark, he went into the cottage. "Ah, there you are!" cried Persyvaunce cheerfully. The little man had been housecleaning, after a fashion. Portions of the floor had been scraped clear, though debris still climbed the multicolored walls like wind-drifted leaves. The table had been entirely cleared and two earthenware plates laid out on it. Persyvaunce, Ryan saw, had used the remains of the egg-tempered orpiment to add a yellow blob to a faded portion of wall. Still wet, it shone there in the nightfall light.

"It doesn't keep," the wizard remarked, seeing Ryan stare.

"Within a day, it stinks." Persyvaunce divided a hot mixture of truffles, asparagus, and chestnuts evenly between the two plates and set an earthenware pot of honey so that it squatted between them. He moved out of the way a smoldering oil lamp, which seemed to cast more shadow than light. With a wave of his hand he invited Ryan to the table.

"A poor dinner, I'm afraid," he said sorrowfully.

"That's all right," said Ryan with American innocence. "Can I have some bread?"

"There isn't any."

Ryan ate with difficulty. He found that he did not like truffles, and the shadows gathering in the corners seemed to gloom away his appetite. Even Persyvaunce's bright walls couldn't keep away the shadows of night. . . . A breeze whisked through the small, unglazed windows into the cottage, making indoors as chilly as outside. Bunches of wild peppermint and wild carrot and wild onion and dried dyestuffs hung down along with the fluttering strips of cloth beneath the thatched roof, startling him with their swayings and rattlings. Strange objects and unidentifiable litter lay everywhere.

"There's alder bark," said Persyvaunce amiably, seeing Ryan staring around. "It makes red of a sort. That mustardy-looking plant is woad." He pointed to identify his materials as he talked. "It gives a fine blue, but it smells appalling. All those kerm bugs give a little bit of red after they're dried and stewed and pressed—but such a little bit! The lichens are for purple. Turnsole gives red or violet *or* blue."

Ryan merely nodded, and Persyvaunce lost his glow of

enthusiasm as he watched the boy pick at his food.

"Perhaps you would have preferred the cuttlefish?" he asked with evident sincerity.

"Not hardly!" But Ryan looked up from his plate. "Mr. Persyvaunce, where did you get the cuttlefish?" He sensed he was not near a seashore. Mountains loomed nearby, and there was no salt smell in the air.

Persyvaunce seemed mildly shocked by the boy's ignorance. "Oh, I magic them up, of course," he explained. "and not always from this world, either. Mercy, I couldn't gather them here! The best colors come from other worlds, and I have found a few of them in my muddleheaded way. Folk come to me from far around for colors. The king himself has sent to me for dyes for his clothing and paints and inks for his workmen and scribes. I have every kind of lead and ocher." The pink-faced wizard beamed with professional pride.

"Though that is not all, of course," he went on more modestly. "Dear me, no, that is the least of it. Color itself is the important thing. It is one of the Deep Magics." Persyvaunce's glance strayed to the plates again. "I do wish potters would put more pleasant colors in earthenware. It is not as if they do not have the means."

"The Deep Magics?" Ryan prodded.

"The Deep Magics. If I learn to know the colors fully, to know them by their most true names and natures, that is to say, if I find the rule of colors—well, then, you see, I shall have the key to all the other worlds. I would be able to send you home with no trouble, lad."

"No hurry," said Ryan. Something ached briefly inside him and made the words hard.

Persyvaunce blinked moistly at him. "I'm a long way from ever doing it, I'm afraid," he said. "Poor lad. I am so very sorry. And your world must be such a very lovely place, full of marvelous colors, what with those—crayons. I must admit, I covet that crayon."

Ryan had forgotten all about it. He reached into the pocket of his jeans and pulled the red thing out. "Here." Impulsively he thrust it at Persyvaunce. "You take it, since you like it so much."

"That's very generous of you," Persyvaunce replied, his voice shaking with emotion. "But I can't take it from you. Do keep it safe. Poor lad, it's the only valuable you have. In this world, it is worth many times its weight in gold."

Ryan gaped at him. "It's just colored wax!"

"What good is gold, except that it shines with its own special color?"

He helped Ryan make himself a bed out of spruce tips and a folded quilt. Ryan lay down in his clothes and pulled another blanket over him. He placed the crayon on a bench near his head. Because of the wizard's abundant sympathy, he felt warm and slept better than he would have believed possible.

Chapter 3

Breakfast turned out to be nothing more than two eggs plus the white of the one Persyvaunce had used for his orpiment, and honey without bread. Persyvaunce's plumpness, Ryan decided, must come from a constant diet of honey and not much more. Already Ryan felt sick of honey.

"We'll have fish for dinner," said Persyvaunce, either reading Ryan's thoughts or responding to his own. "And tomorrow we'd better try to snare a rabbit. Of course people bring bread or potatoes from time to time, to trade for my fine dyes. Certainly. But probably not today."

Ryan looked at him.

"Folk in the village have only just so much use for dyestuffs," Persyvaunce added, lest the boy should form the wrong opinion.

He bustled out to tend the fish, which lived in a small pond at the lower end of the garden, near where the common, or village pastureland, stretched up a long valley to Persyvaunce's holding before giving way to the forest crouching at its back. Ryan watched in disgust while

Persyvaunce dug with his hands in his midden, bringing forth worms for the fish. After feeding them tenderly, the wizard stood appraising his proposed dinner. The fish were not very big. Looking at them, the wizard's hungry, calculating glance melted into a dreamy one. "Such a lavender sheen there about their gills," he murmured. "I wonder, if their scales were ground with linseed oil. . . . No, I've tried that already." He snapped alert. "Shoo!" he yelled, startling Ryan.

A goat was intruding through a gap in the hedge. Ryan and Persyvaunce chased it off. A couple of rabbits flushed from the garden and scampered away as well.

"Pertinacious lapids!" Persyvaunce complained, and to Ryan he remarked, "Once the goats are done with my garden, and the birds, and the bunnies, and the bugs, and the weeds, there's precious little left for me. Perhaps you'd better stay here, lad, and try to fend them all off. I must go work."

Persyvaunce went into the cottage and sat with his eyes closed, and whispered, and chanted, with no results Ryan could see. And thinking back on a meager supper and a meager breakfast, Ryan started weeding young cabbages as if his life depended on it.

"I've been having the strangest dreams about Ryan," said Mr. DeWitt to his wife a few days after the disappearance. "And, Emily, you know I never dream."

"You've never had a son so badly missing before, either," said Mrs. DeWitt. She had developed a strong, wry sense of humor that surprised everyone, even her husband. The problem of Ryan's whereabouts had set the DeWitts to treating each other in different ways. They remained on Magic Island, close to the scene but isolated from their friends and families; they had only each other for support, and they talked more and better than they had for years. Henry DeWitt found himself saying things to his wife that formerly he would not have revealed to anyone.

"You think I'm losing my mind, Em? I get these dreams even in the daytime."

"Daydreams aren't so unusual."

"But these are very vivid, like hallucinations. They block out everything else for a few minutes. It's as if they're coming to me from somewhere else."

Emily DeWitt sat up straight, staring at him with a look he recognized as interest and encouragement. He spoke on.

"I see Ryan as plainly as if he were standing here. His jeans are dirty, and he's working in a funny sort of foreign-looking garden. Did you ever know Ryan to take an interest in gardening?"

"Heavens, no. Nor you."

"And he's chasing goats."

"Good heavens."

"He's chasing them out of the garden, and he yells 'Pertinacious caprids!' at them. Did you ever know Ryan to say something like that?"

"Henry," said his wife softly, "that is so bizarre you could not possibly have thought of it yourself. Where could it be coming from?"

"I don't know. Then I sort of hear something about crayons. I feel sure those blasted crayons had something to do with it, Em." The packet that had been found lying in the street missing the red, he meant.

"That's bizarre, too," said Mrs. DeWitt. "It's been years since Ryan touched a crayon."

"He always had his nose pasted too tight in a book, that's all," grumbled Mr. DeWitt. "Now Emily, please don't say I'm going soft in the head—"

"I think you're doing very well, headwise."

"Thank you. Now. Have you considered bringing in a psychic?"

Within a day it was arranged. The psychic was flown in from New York. She came out to the island, walked around, fingered Ryan's left-behind clothing, the sandy street, and the box of crayons, listened carefully to the air and the DeWitts.

"He's not dead," she told them finally and firmly. "I have searched for so many children who were dead, always sensing they were dead, it is good to know surely that your child is not. He is just where you see him. The garden looks foreign, you say. Why?"

"I'm not sure." Mr. DeWitt fumbled in his mind. "I don't know much about plants and gardens. I guess it just looks—old. The hedge is very tall. The trees are huge, and so are the rosebushes."

"And the forest beyond the garden." The psychic leaned forward. "Does that look foreign, too?"

"Yes. It's like a forest you'd see in a movie."

"What sort of movie?"

"Sort of an adventure movie . . . Robin Hood. Knights in shining armor. That sort of thing."

The psychic nodded and sat back, eyes half-closed. After a while she said, "I think you should go to England."

"How in the world," Mrs. DeWitt wanted to know, "could Ryan have gotten to England?"

"I am not saying he's there. But I have a colleague in England who may be able to help you." The psychic wrote the name and address on a business card for them. "Pay close attention to your dreams, both of you," she advised, and she discussed her fee with them, then left.

Emily DeWitt stayed on Magic Island alone, in case Ryan should somehow come back there. Henry DeWitt took the next available flight to London.

Every day at noontime, if the weather was fine, Ryan and Persyvaunce would take a break in the shade of a big old beech tree and eat bread—for a young woman had brought bread after all, to trade for bright-colored flosses with which to embroider her wedding dress. With a yeasty, full-bellied sense of well-being Ryan and Persyvaunce would eat and talk. Ryan found that he could talk to Persyvaunce as he had never been able to talk to his parents—or, for that matter, anyone else. He liked the wizard. He had never met anyone so kind. Persyvaunce took responsibility for sheltering and protecting him; yet Persyvaunce felt more like a friend to him than any older person had ever been. When the two of them stood side by side and turned their heads, they looked right into each other's eyes.

"I ought to be doing something," Ryan said to the wizard after a few days. "Questing or something." He sensed with a tingling to his bones that Persyvaunce's magical world was made for adventure. He had always wanted adventure, heroism, a life of color, had he not? Yet thus far he had done nothing in this world—so much like the worlds of his daydreams—except eat the wizard's food and tend the wizard's garden. The pattern of a lifetime spent dreaming more than doing was hard to change.

"Looking for the rule of colors, maybe," he added.

The night before, by lamplight, Persyvaunce had at last found his folio, his leather-bound book of magical formulae, under a pile of grapevine to be charred for black. He had opened the volume to show Ryan the chart of correspondences, gloriously illuminated in minium and azure and saffron. It had taken Ryan awhile to read it amid all the flourishes. Persyvaunce had helped him decipher it as follows:

Saturn	*black*	*lead*	*onyx*	*crocodile*
Jupiter	*blue*	*tin*	*sapphire*	*eagle*
Mars	*red*	*iron*	*ruby*	*horse*
Sun	*yellow*	*gold*	*topaz*	*lion*
Venus	*green*	*copper*	*emerald*	*dove*
Mercury	*gray*	*mercury*	*agate*	*swallow*
Moon	*white*	*silver*	*crystal*	*dog*

"It is based on the seven spheres," the wizard had explained, "and for each sphere a color, a metal, a precious gem, and a creature of import."

To Ryan it had looked like nonsense. "The sun isn't a

planet," he declared, "and neither is the moon. And anyway, there are nine planets, not seven. At least in my world," he amended, suddenly realizing that he sounded rude.

Persyvaunce seemed not to mind his lecturing tone. "So this is not the true rule of colors!" the wizard had said excitedly. "I thought not. In some ways it works wonderfully, but in others it doesn't work at all. Dog with moon, bah! And blue with Jupiter, humph. It works for some of my colleagues," Persyvaunce added more calmly, trying to be fair, "but it has never worked properly for me."

Then the wizard had blushed under Ryan's gaze. "Very little works properly for me," Persyvaunce admitted. "Nevertheless . . ." Persyvaunce popped up from his seat and began circling about the cottage. "The true rule of colors must take heed of brown and violet," Ryan heard him mutter. "That much I am sure of."

And ever since, Ryan had been thinking in his slantwise way about the rule of colors, letting colors shimmer and melt in back of his more immediate thoughts. Colors . . . What could be colorful if not adventure? Therefore his quest must be for the rule of colors.

"To get me back to my own world," he added, sitting under the beech tree with Persyvaunce. Though he sounded not too eager about getting back. The thought of the quest itself was what caught at his heart.

And for a wonder Persyvaunce did not laugh at him and his talk of adventuring.

"Indeed you may have to go wandering," Persyvaunce said. "But wait a bit longer. Very soon we should be hearing from the others." The rotund wizard ran his glance over Ryan ruefully. "You need clothing."

"Magic me some," Ryan suggested.

"I can't. Color is my specialty, not garb. I could have outfitted you by magic once," he hastened to add. "But every master wizard has to choose one specialty and give up the rest."

"Huh," Ryan complained. "Who says?"

Persyvaunce blinked. "Why, the college of wizards. That is to say, wizards themselves. Anyone can see that it does no good for a person, wizard or not, to have whatever he wants, lad."

Ryan didn't see. "Why not?"

Persyvaunce's plump, pink face grew serious. "You'd not need to ask," he said in a low voice, "if you'd ever met a warlock."

"Warlock?"

"We call them warlocks. Those who refuse to choose. Those who keep all their powers. They can be terribly dangerous."

Persyvaunce explained, keeping his voice down as if the trees might have ears. Warlocks played at games of power. They dabbled in war, allying themselves with unscrupulous lords. Or they tried to win power for themselves. The realm had been oppressed under several warlock kings in its history, though never for long. Always rebellions arose, or other seekers of power entered the contest, and the warlock kings were killed. Even a warlock could not make himself immortal.

"Who kills them?"

"People likely to become as bad as they. . . . What a terrible mess of death and misery they leave after their play." Persyvaunce's round face had gone stern and sad. "No more, lad."

Reluctantly Ryan turned the talk away from warlocks. "How did you come to choose colors?"

"Why, how would you choose, lad?" Persyvaunce blinked away his sadness and smiled at Ryan. "What is your gift?"

"Huh?"

"I perceive you do not know. I didn't know, either, until I was nearly grown, what I would do."

"My dad plans for me to run his business," said Ryan gloomily. "He's in office supplies. Copiers and stuff. My mom is his bookkeeper."

"Do your parents really hate you?" Persyvaunce inquired so seriously that Ryan bit back his first response and gave the question thought.

"I guess they just sort of disapprove of me," he said after a moment. "They don't seem to like me. Mom doesn't like my clothes. Dad says I read too much."

"But reading is an exalted art!"

"Not where I come from. Dreamer, they call me. My folks say I'm an incredible dreamer."

"You could be a seer or a poet!" Persyvaunce grew excited, and when Ryan looked at him blankly, he demanded, "Aren't poets honored in your world?"

Ryan gazed off toward the forest. Around the corner of the cottage he could see it, the wild, ancient Wilderness of Wirral that stretched away toward bleak mountain peaks.

Meadowlike glades opened between the trees, half-shadowed and half-sunlit, and he found that he was looking for something in their reaches. A rider, perhaps, a king hunting the white stag . . . "I don't think so," he answered Persyvaunce. "I sort of like it better here. Poets—"

He stopped, openmouthed, and jumped up, for a big, sleek russet animal was flickering into sight in the depths of the forest. Too big for a deer, too powerful; it had to be a horse! The rider loomed featureless on its back. Ryan glanced at Persyvaunce. The wizard saw it, too, and had risen to his feet also, peering at the rider in the shadows.

"I don't know him," he said in a low voice to Ryan, "whether he's friend or foe."

The rider drew nearer, out of sight behind the hedge. Then there was a crackling sound; the fellow was urging his horse through the thick of the hedge, snapping branches. Ryan started forward indignantly, but Persyvaunce caught his arm, pressing with his fingers in silent warning. *Caution,* that grip said.

Ryan and Persyvaunce stood still, and the horse walked toward them, straight into the garden, trampling lettuce and leeks and squash vines with its hooves, and the rider halted it in front of where they stood, looking down at them.

He was a lean, handsome young man wearing a sweeping black cloak with a lining of red satin, though the day was warm. His horse stood scarcely less red and gleaming than the satin, its mane in the sunlight so bright that it glowed nearly magenta. A glorious, great-necked, deep-chested animal, mighty of presence, yet with a shapely head and a soft eye—Ryan had dreamed of such horses, and his hands shuddered with his longing to caress it, but the cool gaze of the rider forbade such touch.

"You are Aloysius Persyvaunce, master wizard," the stranger said. "You have lately sent a message for assistance to Grandwizard Durnor." The young man spoke not in inquiry; more in statement. Almost, accusation. His features were hawklike, his eyes dark and keen, his hair as black as his cloak. His tall boots shone bright black over black hose. Something about him reminded Ryan of black-jacketed young men on street corners at home, the sort of youths he would go around the block to stay away from. This stranger was dangerous—or chose to appear dangerous.

"You have the advantage of me, horseman," said Persyvaunce mildly. "I do not know your name."

"It is Rudd."

The visitor offered nothing more but turned his gaze on Ryan. His expression showed nothing. Ryan tried to keep his own face as unreadable, but he felt like stepping back from the glance of those dark eyes. He felt more than afraid—he felt dazed, invaded.

Persyvaunce said with perfect calm courtesy, "That is my guest and assistant, Ryan DeWitt. You wish something of me, Rudd?"

For a moment the youth delayed turning his gaze away from Ryan. Then, with a slowness that seemed nearly insolent, he looked back to Persyvaunce.

"My lord Durnor has received your message," he told the

wizard. "I am his envoy. He has sent me to inquire into the matter and bring word back to him."

Persyvaunce wrinkled his pink brow. "How odd. I have never known Durnor to employ envoys."

"This time he has chosen to do so. I am one of his students, as you once were."

"Ah, I remember you now!" Persyvaunce exclaimed. "I have seen you passing the trays at the congress. Well, you had better get down, hadn't you?" The wizard's frown turned to a smile of easy friendliness.

With only a nod as reply, Rudd dismounted from his majestic horse, tied it to the nearest tree, and followed Persyvaunce into the cottage. Ryan went in, also, but Rudd gave him not another glance.

Chapter 4

While Persyvaunce bustled about preparing the cup of the house for the visitor, Ryan sat still and watched Rudd.

Swiveling his handsome head from side to side, Rudd sent his glance darting around the cottage. From where the stranger sat he could see everything in the small dwelling. And Ryan, unable to believe in his heart that the red crayon was as precious as Persyvaunce said it was, had never moved it from the bench near his bed. Rudd's glance caught on the cylinder of pure, shining, blood-bright red lying in plain sight, and though his face showed nothing, Ryan thought he saw his eyes gleam. Rudd turned and regarded Ryan again as if the boy were not much more than another oddment of the place. Then his roving eyes moved on.

"Here we are!" Persyvaunce hurried to the table with a honey-flavored drink for his guest in a fine glass cup. After Rudd downed it, Persyvaunce offered him a linen napkin dipped in warmed water for his refreshment. Then, the necessary courtesies accomplished, Rudd and the wizard began to talk.

Ryan listened while Persyvaunce explained his predicament, his and Ryan's, to Rudd. And he listened while Rudd questioned and commented and replied. Rudd smiled, and suddenly Ryan felt enchanted. Rudd was charming. His glance no longer seemed hard, but merely keen with interest. His courtesy was the equal of anyone's, and his handsome head and royal bearing made Ryan inclined to like him. Someday he, Ryan, would wear black clothing like Rudd's, so dashing. Perhaps Ryan could go adventuring with this fiery young man. Rudd, though beardless and perhaps not much older than Ryan himself, impressed him as a youth fit to be a hero. Ryan felt ashamed. He had been a fool to think ill of Rudd. Maybe he was not fit to go adventuring with such a noble youth. Maybe he was fit for nothing else but to weed beans. There was the garden to be tended if Persyvaunce was to eat, and maybe he ought to go do it. Though his fascination with Rudd scarcely let him break away, Ryan felt so much abashed by his own scolding thoughts that he got up and drifted outside, leaving Rudd and Persyvaunce to their talk.

Only when Ryan had walked to the end of the garden, well away from Rudd, in the clear air of the outdoors, and saw the handsome chestnut horse pawing unhappily where it stood tied with the bit still in its mouth, did he shake his head and come out of his haze.

"Huh," he said to the horse. "It's been hours, and he's been eating and drinking, but no food and water for you."

Then he thought of how Rudd had glanced at the crayon with gleaming eyes. The day before, an old woman had come up from the village with milk to give Persyvaunce in exchange for a bucket of ruddle dye, and she had exclaimed when she caught sight of the crayon and asked the wizard about it. Other villagers who had come into the cottage had done much the same. Why, then, had Rudd quickly looked away and said nothing?

He remembered also that Rudd had not spoken to him, Ryan, even though Ryan was a visitor from another world. True, the youth's business was with Persyvaunce, but still. . . . "Blooey," said Ryan to himself. "I don't like him, and I don't trust him."

He went back into the cottage and spoke directly to Rudd, looking straight into the young man's flinty eyes, so that Rudd would have to reply to him. "You want me to take care of your horse?"

Rudd's eyes slid away from his, and the youth did not answer.

Persyvaunce spoke up heartily. "By all means, Rudd, let Ryan turn your horse out on the common! You must spend the night. It is not to be considered that you should start back to the college so late in the day."

"Very well." With the grace and power of a rousing peregrine, Rudd got up. "But the boy knows nothing of horses. I'll tend the beast myself." He went out, and Ryan stood at the door, watching him stride away.

"Huh!" Ryan exclaimed after Rudd was out of earshot. "How would he know what I know about horses or anything else?" Though in fact Rudd was right. Ryan had seldom so much as touched a horse.

"Courage, lad." The voice by his shoulder startled him.

Presyvaunce stood there, watching Rudd as Ryan did. "Lord willing, he'll be gone in the morning."

Ryan smiled. So the wizard liked Rudd not much better than he did! But in case Persyvaunce might think he was a jealous child, Ryan said nothing more against Rudd. The visitor was Persyvaunce's houseguest, after all.

And it would have been an insult to Persyvaunce's houseguest and perhaps even Persyvaunce himself for Ryan to hide the crayon or appear to guard it in any way. Where it lay, where a certain round wizard had never so much as touched it, there it must continue to lie.

Rudd seemed not to notice that he ate more than his share of the scanty food at supper. Persyvaunce cheerfully went without. Ryan did the same, silently but not cheerfully. Rudd kept up a spate of charming talk over the meal, but Ryan's growling belly kept him from feeling as enthralled as before. Still, the brief evening had passed, and Ryan was lying in his bed on the floor, half-asleep, before he came awake with a small chill, remembering: Rudd's glinting gaze had caught on the red crayon when he had first entered the cottage.

Persyvaunce had settled down to sleep on the hearth rug at the far end of the room from Ryan, for he had given Rudd his bed. Rudd lay between Ryan and Persyvaunce. In no way could Ryan consult with the wizard without Rudd's seeing and hearing.

I must stay awake all night, he decided.

It was harder than it sounded. He felt tired. At first the excitement of the vigil kept him awake; this at last was adventure! His heart pounded at every slight noise and stirring in the night. Later, he pushed his blanket to one side so that the nip of the night air would keep him from sleeping, and so that he would not tangle in it if he had to move suddenly. Adventure seemed not to matter nearly as much as rest. . . . In spite of all he could do, sleep started creeping into his head, making his eyes close and his mind feel fuzzy. He thought he was thinking when already he was dreaming. Why stay awake for just a crayon? He could go to the store and get another box of them tomorrow. A crayon was a thing of no value. Who in the world would want to steal one from him?

Which world?

He blinked and pulled himself awake again. Who would steal such a thing? Rudd, that's who, he told himself fiercely. And Rudd was not going to have it. Even though it was just colored wax. Ryan kept himself awake by repeating the name of the person he distrusted inside his mind. Rudd, Rudd, red, red ruddy crayon, Rudd—

Rudd was moving.

Ryan stiffened. The cottage was dark, much darker than any place he had ever slept in his own world, where street lamps and city lights, house lights and headlights fogged the air with a faint glow everywhere. No such glow came here. Even the embers in the hearth lay hidden beneath ashes. He could see nearly nothing. Still, he could hear the faint rustlings from Rudd's bed, sense the moving of a shadow. Rudd was coming.

Ryan knew he was coming. He couldn't prove it, but he

knew. The boy lay rigid, panic turning him wet with sudden sweat, for the first time aware of real danger. Suppose Rudd was a cutthroat? It might not be just a matter of grabbing the crayon and calling out. Yet, he couldn't do anything until—

A loud yell jolted the night, and a blundering noise from the direction of the hearth, and a clang of metal. Ryan sprang up. "Mr. Persyvaunce!" he cried.

"Ah! Oh! Oh, dear," huffed Persyvaunce. "I believe I've rolled into the fire!"

He had, for the faint glow of embers showed where ashes had been pushed away. And in that dull red light Ryan caught a glimpse of quick movement. Rudd was just slipping back into his bed. As long as he stayed there, the crayon was safe.

Persyvaunce got up clumsily, rattling the poker and firedog he had knocked over. "Oh, dear," he said again.

"Did you burn yourself?" Ryan exclaimed, running over to him.

"Not really. Just enough to awaken me. Stir up the fire, lad, and make a light so we can deal with this mess."

"No need," said Rudd sourly from his bed, and he held up one hand. Yellow flames wavered on his fingertips, lighting the cottage like a lamp. Ryan stood openmouthed, but Persyvaunce exclaimed joyfully, "Oh, very good! I forgot you were still a student. Oh, dear." The latter because he could now see the ashes and soot that blackened the hearth rug, the floor, and his own patched tunic. Ryan tried to brush him off. Persyvaunce stopped him with a gesture.

"It's no use, lad. We'd be up half the night, trying to clear away this mess. We'll deal with it tomorrow." Persyvaunce stepped to a clean patch of floor and stripped off the soiled tunic, standing pink and pudgy in his smallclothes.

"Rudd," he said to his guest, "I very much fear that I am going to have to climb in with you. It will be crowded, but the night is chill."

A fleeting look of disgust crossed Rudd's handsome face. But there was little he could say by way of dissent, for the bed was Persyvaunce's, after all. And there was nowhere else for either of them to go, not even a stable. "Of course," said Rudd with ill grace. He could not expect to get up to prowl the night without rousing Persyvaunce. He had been bested.

Turning away from Rudd a moment to toss his sooty tunic in a corner, Persyvaunce caught Ryan's eye and winked.

Ryan went at once back to his bed, for relief and laughter were tugging at the corners of his mouth, and he did not want Rudd to see him smile. Near his head lay the red crayon. The room went dark again, and Ryan went to sleep.

In the morning, after a cold breakfast, Rudd caught his magnificent red horse and went on his way with short farewells. Ryan stopped sweeping soot long enough to stand at the door and watch him ride off into the forest. Persyvaunce stood beside him.

"Did you really roll into the fire," Ryan asked him, "and burn yourself?" Persyvaunce gave him a quiet smile.

"No, lad. I was lying awake and waiting for him to make his move, just as you were."

Rudd had ridden well away, out of sight and out of earshot. Ryan looked at Persyvaunce's twinkling eyes and thought how thoroughly the small, round wizard had befooled dashing, black-clad Rudd, and he laughed out loud, all the laughter he had stifled in the night bursting out of him, shout after shout of laughter. Merrily Persyvaunce laughed with him.

"Oh!" gasped the wizard, short of breath. "Oh! I must say, it was fun."

"I was scared," Ryan admitted in the midst of his laughter, and Persyvaunce sobered.

"As well you might be. We know nothing of yonder youngster, but I do not like what I sense. Are you sure you are not acquainted with him, lad?"

The question seemed as laughable to Ryan as Rudd's defeat. "How could I be?"

"Of course, it is nonsensical. Still—I sense. . . ." Persyvaunce's gray-eyed gaze had gone distant and intent. Ryan grew as still as the look on the little man's face.

"What makes you think I might know Rudd?" he asked quietly.

"A—a connection, a linkage . . . I sense something between the two of you. Something like the uneasy bonds between iron and ruby, or moon and dog," the wizard tried to explain, "in the chart of correspondences."

Ryan stared at Persyvaunce with narrowed eyes, trying to comprehend. The little wizard quirked a smile at him.

"I don't understand it, either, lad. I invited Rudd to stay the night because I wanted to see what was what with him. And I still know little enough. Though it's plain the fellow lied. He cannot be an envoy of Durnor's. Count the days." Persyvaunce reckoned on his fingers. "My message to Durnor cannot have reached him more than three days ago. Rudd cannot have come here in that time, unless his horse has wings." The wizard turned a thoughtful look on Ryan. "In fact, if he traveled as swiftly as he was able, he must have started here before I sent the vellums. Or at the very latest, that same day. The day you arrived, lad."

Ryan said slowly, "But why did he come here? Is he stupid? He must know you know he lied."

"And he seems anything but stupid. It must be that he does not care what we think, Ryan. As to why he came here: I wish I could say."

Ryan said nothing. He no longer felt like laughing. An uneasy sense was growing in him that he had a powerful enemy, and the thought chilled him.

"Something odd is afoot," said Persyvaunce softly, "odd and awry, and I wish I knew what it was."

The address the psychic had given Ryan's father turned out to be far out in Cheshire, and there was no telephone listing for the man, a Mr. A. P. Chelon of Beeswale Cot, Wirral. After a long drive in a rented car through a bewilderment of country roads, Mr. DeWitt finally located Beeswale Cot in the late afternoon.

He got out of his car, stretched wearily, then stood looking around him with a faint frown. The garden seemed somewhat like the one in his dream. A tall hedge, beehives ranged along it—but they were white-painted wooden beehives, not the old-fashioned basket sort. A few huge trees stood, but the forest was a mere coppice. Beans climbed up bamboo poles. Hollyhocks and foxglove spired up the sides of a squat cottage that, also, looked familiar, though the roof was slate shingled, not thatched.

"Well," Mr. DeWitt muttered to himself, noting the huge, sprawling rosebushes, "there must be lots of gardens like this." He walked up the pebble path between herb gardens and plots of cabbages, past a birdbath where bees drank, to the heavy oak door. A brass knocker in the shape of a turtle adorned it. He knocked.

When the door opened, a small, round, pink-faced man peered out at Mr. DeWitt from behind thick glasses. Mr. Chelon was so short that Henry DeWitt looked down on him. The little man's wispy hair barely covered his scalp, which glowed as pink as his face. He wore trousers patched at the knees for gardening and a moth-ravaged brown sweater. Mr. DeWitt felt not at all confident about him.

"Mr. Chelon?"

"At your service."

"Are you a psychic?"

"Dear me, I don't think so. I am a sort of student of the obscure, I suppose." Over Mr. A. P. Chelon's shoulder, Henry DeWitt could see an impressively untidy room. The man was a bachelor, by the looks of things. "You have come to consult me?" Mr. Chelon seemed scarcely able to believe it. "How good of you. Let us sit and talk in the garden. It is far more pleasant than the house."

Sourly Mr. DeWitt agreed and took a seat with Mr. Chelon on a bench under a huge beech tree. He felt annoyed, as if he had wasted his time coming here. Days wasted. He would state his business as briefly as possible and cut his losses. But when he began to talk, looking into that soft and serious face, he felt his annoyance give way to a dim, illogical hope.

Mr. Chelon was wonderful to talk to. The little man listened to his account of Ryan's disappearance with full attention and few interruptions, never thrusting forward his own opinions or advice, but sometimes offering a quiet, courteous sort of sympathy. So comforting did Henry Dewitt find him that he talked far longer than he had intended. The sun had set and the sky had turned nearly dark before he noticed that it was getting late.

The unreasoning hope could not be silenced any longer. He put the question to Mr. Chelon.

"Can you help me find my son?"

"Certainly I will try," the small man replied promptly. Mr. Dewitt did not like the sound of "try," though what more could he reasonably expect? He pressed the question.

"What do you plan to do?"

"I cannot yet tell. We must talk more. Tomorrow."

Talk gagged Ryan's father. He felt frantic for action of some sort. But what? He could not tell what to do, any more than Mr. Chelon could.

"Well," he said gruffly, "I had better find myself some supper and a place to stay. Is there an inn nearby?"

"No reason you should not stay right here in the cottage with me," said the other. "It's cluttered, I know. Worse than a bear pit, in fact. But no harm in that, and you're welcome. Who knows; some good might come of it." A. P. Chelon looked out over the tops of his glasses with friendly, anxious, blue-gray eyes. And as the little man said, why not?

"Thank you," said Mr. DeWitt. "I'll stay."

"I feel that we ought to be doing something," Persyvaunce said to Ryan as they sat under their tree the following noontime, "but I'm not at all sure what."

"About Rudd?"

"About you and that red talisman of yours, to keep you both safe from Rudd or whatever is on the move." Persyvaunce looked very worried. "Oh, if only I weren't such a nincompoop. I don't know where to start, but we can't wait any longer to hear from the others."

Ryan had stopped listening, for something in the sky had caught his eye. He pointed upward. "Look!"

A large square of vellum came flapping over the treetops and skittered down to land like a falcon on Persyvaunce's arm. Startled, the wizard ogled at it a moment before he took it in his hands.

"A congress of wizards!" he exclaimed. He passed the vellum, which now lay flat and still, to Ryan. On it, painted in dull red, Ryan saw a circle made up of many smaller circles converging on a central hub. "Red, yet!" declared Persyvaunce, looking alarmed. "And that was sent by Durnor's hand, unquestionably. We must go at once."

"You mean—the red color is for danger, and each little circle is a wizard like you, and—"

"Yes, lad, yes! We are all to come. The others live closer; they will be waiting. Hurry, now, pack your things!"

There was not much packing to be done. Ryan picked up his crayon and shouldered the sack of food that Persyvaunce had hastily bundled up for him. Persyvaunce threw a few pans and oddments into his own bag. They each rolled a quilt to sleep on. Then they went out and latched the cottage door. The wizard looked around him for a moment, as if saying a silent good-bye to his garden before leaving it to the goats. Then, at a more rapid pace than Ryan would have thought possible, the round little man set off, through a gap in the hedge and into the forest, with the boy hurrying after him.

Chapter 5

"Will we be in this forest all the way?" Ryan asked before the first day was over. Clay-green shadows lay heavy on him, seeming to crawl on his back, and he heard strange, howling noises in the directionless distance. For no reason that he could put into words he kept turning his head to look behind him. The trees loomed immense all around, and the track Persyvaunce followed seemed narrow and frail. Nothing in the wilderness had hurt Ryan or threatened him, yet it seemed to him that he had never set foot in any place so fearsome.

"It is formidable, is it not?" Persyvaunce acknowledged, replying to Ryan's unspoken words first. "No, not all the way. Only the first few days."

"Only," Ryan muttered. It had started to rain, and the wet dripped down even through the thick leaves. It made the forest look dreary as well as fearsome. "Brown, brown, brown," he grumbled at a tree trunk.

"Brown!" Persyvaunce looked around at him, mildly shocked. "Why, surely you can see that it's any color but brown! Look again."

Ryan was startled into staring at the trunk of a towering oak as if he had never seen a tree in his life.

"It's puce, and pearly gray, and dusky pink or green with lichen, and charcoal black where it's wet, and sepia still from springtime," said Persyvaunce more gently. "Brown! Is that the way people see in your world? You'll be telling me that apples are red, next."

Ryan knew that in crayoning coloring books he had always made apples red and tree trunks brown. "Maybe," he said. "Is it the rule of colors to see things another way?"

Persyvaunce looked at him thoughtfully and did not reply.

Just before dark he and Persyvaunce stopped and gathered plenty of deadwood for a fire. The wizard brought flint out of his bag and struck it against the back of his steel knife blade. "There's a knack to it," he told Ryan, as Ryan could see there was. But all the wood was sodden from the rains and drenching dews of that place. Though Persyvaunce shredded punk wood fine and struck the flint until sparks settled on it thick as starlings on corn, it would not light.

"I thought at first I had forgotten the flint," lamented Persyvaunce, "and now it seems I might as well have."

"Can't you start a fire with your hand, as Rudd did?"

"I could once, lad, when I was a student. We wizards try all things as students. But fire starting was one of the powers I left behind when I Chose." Persyvaunce drew breath for a titanic effort, then clashed the flint fiercely against the knife blade. Sparks showered down like orange leaves in autumn. A thread of smoke wisped up.

"All right!" Ryan exclaimed. "Rudd couldn't have done it any better."

"Rudd would set his tunic hem on fire?" inquired Persyvaunce gloomily, smothering the spark with his hands.

"It's an idea," said Ryan, crestfallen, but Persyvaunce brightened immediately and began pulling threads from the ragged edges of his clothing, searching for places where his body heat had kept it dry. Ryan added lint from inside his jeans pockets. They laid this fresh tinder in a small, fragile pile atop the punk wood, and once again Persyvaunce struck flint to steel. This time a tiny fire snake-tongued its way out of the kindling and slowly grew until it was large enough to devour the wettest bough.

"Whew," Ryan sighed. "I would have hated to be without a fire in this woods at night."

He and Persyvaunce sat side by side and watched the fire beckon and sway and draw ruddy sparkles out of the wet, black wilderness.

"Speaking of Rudd," said Persyvaunce quietly, though no one had spoken of Rudd very recently, "we had better sleep by turns, Ryan, and keep a watch."

Ryan nodded. He, too, had seen the hoofprints on the narrow, loamy trail. Rudd had come this same way, and not very long before them. If for any reason he had ridden slowly, he might be near at hand.

They ate a little bread. Ryan did not feel very hungry. He slept first, lightly, hearing howlings in the ebony-black woods all around. And the wolves, he knew, might be less dangerous than Rudd. In his uneasy dreaming, Rudd was a brigand crazed by desire for something more treasured than gold.

The crayon lay in one of the bags, wrapped in Persyvaunce's spare tunic, for Ryan felt afraid to keep it in his jeans pocket now that he understood how valuable it was, in case the movements of his body might break it. But in his dream, he wore it like a talisman around his neck, on a golden chain, and Rudd tried to wrench it away, strangling Ryan with the chain. He felt the metal cutting into his neck—

He woke up, jarred awake by the dream, and found nothing more fearsome than Persyvaunce nodding by the fire.

Later, when it came his turn to take his watch, he kept hearing faint sounds behind the cracklings of the fire, the sounds of something moving in the blackness beyond, but never loud enough that he could be sure of them. He felt no inclination to sleep. Fear held his eyes wide open, though he told himself he was imagining things. Once he thought he saw the reddish shine of two watching eyes beyond the fire. When he moved his head to look again, they were gone.

"Do wolves' eyes shine red in the firelight?" he asked Persyvaunce in the morning.

"No! Green." As he had thought, Persyvaunce knew the answer at once to a question of color. "A sort of liquid green, like seawater."

Ryan said nothing more.

That day, walking, he saw a redbird fly across the forest path, through a shaft of sunlight, looking more fluorescent pink than red in the sunshine, Ryan thought. The small act of seeing pleased him. For the next hour or more he passed the plodding time looking for colors to notice. . . .

His skin went cold. A flash of russet far away beneath the trees. As he tried to point it out to Persyvaunce, it was gone.

"A deer?" the wizard asked quietly.

"Maybe." Ryan hoped so but burst out, "It looked just the color Rudd's horse did when I first saw it in the forest."

"And you saw eyes in the night." Though Ryan had not said so. "It may be, lad, that our fire we were so glad to have has led Rudd straight to us." Persyvaunce shrugged, his expression whimsical. But Ryan noticed that the wizard kept an alert gaze moving around the forest, down the glades that opened between the huge, ivy-covered oaks and elms, down the sketchy trail both behind and ahead. Rudd might be anywhere, if he was stalking them.

That night, though no less damp than before, they sat down at dusk, settled themselves stolidly in the wet, arranged their bags and quilts, ate bread and cheese, and watched night take the wilderness. No moon shone overhead; not even stars, for the sky hung clouded with fog and unshed rain. Persyvaunce waited until everything had turned as black as Rudd's black velvet tunic; then he nudged Ryan. Silently the two of them got up and gathered their baggage. Persyvaunce felt for Ryan's hand in the darkness, found it. Holding hands so that they would not become separated, the two of them felt their way along as quietly as they could, sliding their feet so as not to step on a twig, balancing their quilts on their shoulders and feeling for trees with their free hands. They intended to move well away from the place where Rudd thought they would be.

They stayed on the trail, or so they hoped. To either side of it stood trees, thorn bushes, rustling bracken. As long as they could find a clear space to walk in, they hoped it was the trail. But many times they blundered, backtracked, tried again. The night seemed full of confusion and groping branches. Every rock in their way made them wonder in panic if they had lost the trail. For the Wilderness of Wirral was immense; a pair of wanderers could flounder about in it until they starved, never finding a way out. Losing the trail would be as bad as falling prey to Rudd.

At last, after what seemed a long time—though they probably had come no farther than the next bend of the path—Persyvaunce stopped and whispered to Ryan, very softly, "Good enough."

Ryan nodded, though Persyvaunce could not see him nod. Rudd would find it no easier than they had to move about in the night, unless he made a light with his hands. "I'll take the first watch," Ryan whispered.

Persyvaunce did not argue but lay down where he was, bundled himself into his quilt as quietly as he could, laid his head on his bag, and went to sleep.

Ryan sat up and held his eyes wide open, though there was nothing to see but blackness. He moved his head slowly in all directions, like an owl, scanning the forest. There was all too much to hear, and he could make no sense of it: howlings, hootings, screamings, rustlings, stirrings of branches and leaves. Small rodents ran close at hand; their every movement startled him. His eyes strained, trying to find form in the darkness—

When at last he saw something, he did not at first believe it but thought that his overweary eyes were befooling him, making sparks and glimmers of light in the night. Then he blinked and grew sure. Moving nothing but his hand, he reached over and gripped Persyvaunce hard to awaken and caution him.

The little wizard felt the message of danger in that touch and sat up at once, without even a sleepy sound. And by the way Persyvaunce came to rigid attention, Ryan could tell that he saw it also.

At not too great a distance, beyond trees, someone's uplifted hands made a dim yellow fire.

Ryan felt Persyvaunce's pudgy finger against his lips, cautioning him not to speak. Within the moment, the flicker of fire wavered out as if it had never been. If he had felt himself anywhere near sleep, Ryan could almost have believed he had dreamed it. But there was no sleep in him. He felt more awake than he ever had in his life, tingling with awareness of everything around him. He sensed as much as heard Rudd's circlings and searchings through the forest, now near, now far; he followed the young man's movements with the movements of his own head. He grew less afraid—though no less alert—for unless Rudd made a light again, he was not likely to find them without blundering right into them.

Which he nearly did. He walked past them little more than an arm's length away, and Ryan and Persyvaunce sat silent as young rabbits in the nest, letting him pass. They sat that way until daylight, and daylight showed them the trail a little more than an arm's length away, where Rudd had walked. They had wandered just off it.

"One more night like this, lad," Persyvaunce said to Ryan once they were on their way again, "and then we will be out of this forest and staying at inns."

Ryan nodded cheerfully enough. He did not feel tired, though he had just spent a night with no sleep at all. He felt energetic, almost feverish.

"When he made the light with his hands," he said, "that must have been where he thought we should be. Where we had stopped earlier."

"Undoubtedly," Persyvaunce agreed.

"He was so surprised we weren't there. . . ." Ryan left the sentence unfinished and started laughing.

"Indeed he was astonished," said Persyvaunce. "He couldn't believe it until he had made a light and seen with his eyes, which was very unwise of him, if he wanted to come on us with stealth." But Persyvaunce did not laugh.

"Which was why he didn't bother sneaking afterwards." Ryan smothered his laughter, but he could not help grinning. He and Persyvaunce had fooled Rudd again.

But they had no plan for the night to come.

After dark they moved their camp again, farther than they had before, though they risked losing the trail. And, as Persyvaunce had said in a low voice toward the end of the day, they could not expect the same trick to work twice. But having no other thoughts as to a ruse, he felt they had to try it, then keep a sharp watch.

Persyvaunce took the first turn at guard. He felt that Ryan needed sleep. Ryan did not feel sleepy until he lay down, but then sudden exhaustion overtook him, and he slept restlessly, with twitching legs, as if running from something.

When the midnight world burst apart, it was as if a nightmare had exploded out of his uneasy dreams.

He awoke already screaming, and there it hovered over him, huge, mushrooming, fiery white, with bits of human bodies oozing from it, bodies blown to scum, turning liquid and frying in that terrible, searing heat—and he was shrieking, running, wildly fleeing though he knew it was no use, for no one could escape once that deadly final monster was loosed. Ryan ran until something hit him hard. Then he fell, unconscious.

When he awoke, it was daylight, and trees stood coldly all around him.

He staggered up, groaning, confused. His head hurt. He felt at it with his fingertips. A sizable lump on his forehead—had someone hit him? Where was Persyvaunce? Nothing but wilderness anywhere in sight. No trail, no friendly pink-faced wizard. Ryan was alone.

Panic prickled in him, and not only because he was lost. For a moment he felt sure Persyvaunce lay dead, swallowed by the mushroom-cloud monster, torn to bits, liquified. Weeping welled up in him, he felt so sure. But why was the forest still standing?

Angrily he held back his tears. It was Rudd who had done this thing. He had Rudd to reckon with. Perhaps

Persyvaunce lay hurt, hit on the head, as he had been. If so, Rudd would pay, somehow.

But knowing he was in no condition to take on Rudd at the time, he didn't dare shout. He cast about in circles, searching, finding nothing but woods and more woods. As day wore on toward noontime, he gave up feeling vengeful toward Rudd or afraid of him. All he wanted was to find Persyvaunce. More even than he wanted to find food, or the trail, or a way out of this bewildering forest, he wanted to find his friend, and know that the little wizard was all right, and not be alone any longer, so utterly alone in a strange, dangerous world. . . . Tears hung in his eyes, and he no longer cared who or what heard him. He gathered breath to call out—

Wait. Rustling. His heart stopped for fear that it was Rudd.

Then a clumsy snapping of twigs sounded, and far off in the forest a round little man in clownish clothing came in view.

"Mr. Persyvaunce!" Ryan shouted, a cry of joy that rang out through the wilderness.

"Ryan! My dear boy, are you all right?"

He ran toward the wizard. In a moment they met and threw their arms around each other, and Ryan was crying, but he didn't care. He had seen tears on the wizard's pink face. Gratefully he sagged for a moment against Persyvaunce's ample body.

"I was afraid you were hurt," he said when he could speak.

"Not a bit. But you are." Persyvaunce held him by the shoulders, wincing in sympathy as he studied the bruise on Ryan's forehead. "Who or what hit you?"

"I'm not sure. I was running from—from some sort of monster."

"Yes, I saw it, the demon out of the pit!" Persyvaunce shuddered, and utmost terror shadowed his gentle face for a moment. "Black as the bowels of earth, and immense, and clawed. Don't ask me how I saw it in the nighttime, but I did."

Ryan gawked at him in bewilderment. "But it was not black at all!" he cried. "It was white fire, and—and a sort of nuclear bomb thing, except it was full of blood."

Persyvaunce stared back, and his face went bleak as he understood. "Rudd has befooled us this time, and mightily," he said.

"I knew it," said Ryan. "When I woke up, I knew it had to be Rudd."

"We were gulled by a wizard's trick. He touched our minds somehow and made us each see the thing we most dreadfully feared." Persyvaunce sighed and shrugged. "Well, let us go, lad. I blundered across the trail a while ago, back this way." He turned and led Ryan across the leaf-littered ground.

They found the trail and, in time, their campsite. Their bags lay emptied and thrown aside, their belongings scattered, their food trampled into the ground. The pouch of money Persyvaunce had brought with him was missing. And so was Ryan's crayon.

Chapter 6

We've been badly bested," said Persyvaunce quietly, looking as grim as Ryan had ever seen him. Ryan did not like to see him look so beaten.

"It doesn't matter," he told him. "I'm glad just to be back with you. Really."

Persyvaunce smiled like sunrise. "You're right, lad. It could be far worse. We've found each other, and we've found the trail. But it does matter, about the red talisman." He gave Ryan a serious, level look. "It was yours."

"And the money was yours. So what are we going to do?"

By way of answer Persyvaunce started gathering up gear and what food he could salvage. "For the time," he said, "we are going to move fast, if we do not wish to spend yet another night in this wretched forest."

Persyvaunce moved so fast that Ryan had to trot to keep up with him. The wizard had never walked slowly, not since the beginning of the journey, but now he twinkled along at an amazing rate. Ryan grew footsore at the pace he set and wondered if Persyvaunce would lose weight.

Through afternoon and through dusk into nightfall they traveled without stopping and without much talk. And Ryan had just decided with an inward groan that they would be spending one more night in the Wilderness of Wirral after all, when he saw ahead a slightly lighter patch of gloom, asphalt gray rather than black. In a few more moments he and Persyvaunce stepped out of forest onto a benighted meadow, a common. Under the open sky there was light enough to see by, even though flossy clouds veiled the stars. Persyvaunce led on until the forest lay well behind, then stopped with a tired sigh and dropped to the ground where he stood.

Ryan sat beside him as they silently shared what little food they had. Ryan felt too tired to care that it was so little. Persyvaunce cared, though not for his own sake.

"That's all there is, lad," he said sorrowfully. "And no money now, either, for stopping at inns, however cheaply."

"Blast that Rudd," Ryan said.

"No use blasting him at present," said Persyvaunce. "He's well away by now, on his fine fox-red horse. And we'll be begging at kitchen doors for bread and a pallet in the cow shed."

The next day would be soon enough to face that, Ryan judged. He yawned but said, "I'll take the first watch," since Persyvaunce had taken it the night before.

"But we can't afford the time to beg," the wizard went on as if he had not heard. "We must come to the congress quickly. Likely most of the others are already there."

"How many more days will it take us?"

"Six or seven, on shank's mare. More at a starving pace. Ryan, may I never have more pressing occasion to call for help. No, lad, you sleep. I am going to sit here and send for aid."

"Huh? How?"

"In much the same way as I send for crayons and the like." The little wizard had slumped where he sat until he resembled a deflated kickball. "And the results are likely to be just as happenstance. Ryan, I am sorry. Here you are, and it's my fault—"

"I'm glad to be here," Ryan told him.

"You're so kind to say so." In the darkness Ryan heard Persyvaunce sniffle. "But you can't be glad to be set upon and starving, and I—I can't promise you anything. Of all the wizards who ever were, I must be the worst."

Ryan reached over and touched the little man's hand. "Of all the wizards I ever met, you're the best," he said.

"I have been having the most compelling, extraordinary dreams," Mr. DeWitt told his host, Mr. Chelon. "They started yesterday evening while I was still awake and kept up most of the night."

"About your son?"

"About Ryan. I saw him as clearly as I see you. He was wearing the same clothes as when he—when I saw him last, but they are getting dirty and ragged. And he looked thin, and pale, and there was a big bruise on his forehead. He looked—" Mr. DeWitt stopped and swallowed. "He looked like a waif. His hair was plastered to his head in strings, from sweat or rain or something, and he was lying asleep on the grass, on some sort of old blanket or quilt."

"Asleep, you say?" Mr. Chelon seemed surprised.

"Yes. But there was someone sitting next to him, by his head. A man I've never seen before. He looked—well, Mr. Chelon, he reminded me of you." Henry DeWitt glanced at Mr. Chelon to gauge his reaction, but Mr. Chelon seemed not at all surprised. "He looked a good bit like you, except that he wore some odd sort of clothes. Made me think of Friar Tuck in the old Robin Hood movies."

"Yes, it's my counterpart in that world," Mr. Chelon said quietly. "He's the one who's sending you the dreams, then."

"What?" Mr. DeWitt half rose from his armchair in his agitation. "What are you saying?"

"I'll explain soon. First, tell me what else you saw."

"Really, that was all, except that the—the Friar Tuck fellow, you know—he looked down at Ryan from time to time, watching him sleep. The rest of the time he mostly stared straight ahead. Then later, after I went to sleep myself, I had a lot of confused dreams about Ryan walking through a forest and running in the night and being chased by someone on a big red horse, I don't know who."

"I think you should take comfort," Mr. Chelon said, "that my counterpart has befriended the boy."

"Would you tell me what you're talking about!"

It was not going to be easy to convince this big, practical-minded businessman that his son had somehow slipped into another world. Mr. Chelon looked out at him earnestly from behind his glasses and did his best.

"And if Ryan has found a friend in this rotund fellow you mention," he concluded, "you may think I flatter myself, Mr. DeWitt, but it's a very good thing. Even from my distant dealings with him I'd say the chap is decent and very tenderhearted. He'll want only what is best for the boy. You can depend on it, he is trying his hardest to return the youngster to his home world."

Mr. Dewitt looked back at him for several moments, saying absolutely nothing, his face hard and blank.

"Unfortunately," Mr. Chelon added under that scrutiny, "he is also a bit unscientific in his methods. Nevertheless, I cannot help feeling the news is good."

Mr. DeWitt continued to stare until evidently he made up his mind about something.

"Mr. Chelon," he said at last, "assuming the case is as you say, what can I do to help get Ryan back?"

"We must talk more," said Mr. Chelon. "I do not yet know."

"Talk!" Mr. DeWitt burst out, lunging up from his chair, protesting as he had not protested at the mention of other worlds. "Talk is cheap, Mr. Chelon. We must do something!"

"My dear fellow!" exclaimed the little man with such ardent compassion that Mr. DeWitt slowly sat down again.

Later, Henry DeWitt went to his room and wrote to his wife. "Dear Emily," he told her, "I consider myself a good judge of character, and I have decided to trust Mr. Chelon.

I feel sure he is not trying to swindle me. He strikes me as a principled person who genuinely wants to help, and he has not even mentioned fee. Please don't think I am losing my marbles."

After the body of the letter he added, "P.S. Em, I only hope Mr. Chelon is able to help. There is no way I can judge whether he is competent."

Ryan awoke in the morning to find Persyvaunce still seated but nodding over him. He roused the wizard. "Mr. Persyvaunce," he accused, "you didn't wake me for a turn at watch."

"You look the better for the sleep, lad." Persyvaunce, however, looked tired. His mouth smiled, but his eyes did not. He got up slowly, stiffly, like an old man.

"Did you find us any help?" Ryan asked, knowing at once that he should not have. The question bowed Persyvaunce's shoulders like a burden.

"There's no way I can tell for sure, Ryan. I—"

Mouth still open as if to speak, the little wizard fell silent, and Ryan, following his gaze, gaped as well. Just coming over the mountaintops on the horizon, an enormous bird flew toward them—or soared, rather, for its wings scarcely moved. Ryan found it hard to judge size at the distance, but he knew he had never seen a bird so large in his own world. And the sunlight flashed off it as if it were made of gold.

"Ho—ly!" he gasped when he had caught his breath. "What is it?"

Persyvaunce answered without turning his eyes away from the sky. "An eagle."

"Eagles are that big here?"

"Only a few."

It swooped closer, a gilded raptor against a sky as blue as rare lapis lazuli. It circled near, then seemed to sight them where they stood alone on the open uplands. With the speed of a striking hawk it flew straight toward them, and Ryan flinched with fear. The fierce curved beak, meant to rip, the talons, sharp as scimitars and almost large enough to pick him up—what if the eagle intended to pounce on him? Did such birds do that to humans here? It seemed possible, and there was nowhere to run, nowhere to hide on the grassy hilltop. But Persyvaunce did not seem afraid. Ryan stood still by his side.

The eagle circled overhead, huge, the size of a horse with wings longer than two tall men with two long lances. Then it plummeted to land and thudded down a small distance in front of them. It stared at them with distant yellow eyes over its hard, bony beak, and Persyvaunce stared back.

"Confound it," he complained, "Durnor knows I never ride the things. He's done this just to annoy me. Or, truth to tell, to scare me silly." He turned to Ryan, and the boy saw that he was, indeed, afraid. "What do you say, lad? This is our help. Are you game?"

"We have to—to ride it?"

"Or else beg our way to the congress and look like fools when we finally draggle in."

The eagle stood still, waiting, watching their deliberations with a look of scorn or boredom.

"Will it—will it dump us?"

Persyvaunce considered, then smiled almost gleefully. "You do have a way of cutting right to the core of things, Ryan!" he exclaimed. "No, it won't dump us. So why am I afraid? Come on. We really have no choice."

He marched up to the eagle, which lay down on the ground as if on a nest to receive him. Awkwardly, ruffling the bronze-bright feathers of its neck, he settled himself in front of its wings. Ryan climbed on right behind him and clutched him tightly around the chest. The eagle felt odd under him, pillowed with down and slick with feathers and bony.

"You're shaking, lad."

Ryan nodded. His jaws had clenched too tightly to let him talk.

"Get down. I'll go and send someone for you. Or, let me see, a message—"

Violently Ryan shook his head, clutching tighter. Terrified he might be, but he would not be separated from Persyvaunce again.

"You're right. It's no good. We have to go together."

The eagle, feeling them seated on its back and shoulders, rose to its two great clawed feet, and Persyvaunce became as agitated as Ryan.

"Hold on to me if you must, lad, but for all sakes' sake don't unbalance me," he babbled. "There's nothing for me to hang on to, and these slippery feathers—"

"Pass your belt around its neck," Ryan interrupted, suddenly finding his voice.

It was too late. With slow, powerful strokes of its mighty

wings, the eagle rose into the air. Persyvaunce squeaked once, then fell silent.

"Why, lad, this is not so bad after all!" he exclaimed a moment later, with relief.

It wasn't. The eagle flew as smoothly as a boat gliding through still water, keeping its wings level. And Persyvaunce rode like a weight anchored to the eagle's back, his legs curled around its shoulders and gripping its breast; like a beanbag full of lead shot, with his round bottom embracing the contours of his feathered mount; like an egg-shaped doll that wouldn't fall down. Holding onto the wizard's chest, Ryan slowly let out his breath and relaxed.

"My stars, the colors!" Persyvaunce cried.

Below them lay meadows misted with the white and pink and yellow of early-summer flowers blooming in great patches of color. Ahead lay the blunt-topped, gray-green mountains with their heathery moors. Even Ryan sat spellbound by the colors of the moors, for he had never seen any.

"The water!" Persyvaunce marveled, looking down on a lake caught in a mountain's lip. "Truly as blue as sky, from up here."

They both sat rapt on the eagle's back as the great bird bore them over the mountains. Ryan saw sheep on an upland meadow like white potato bugs—he could not make out their legs, even as they ran from the eagle's shadow. Maybe they're on wheels, and I don't know it, he joked with himself. This is a strange world. Then he saw fallow deer grazing near a stream, seeming somehow as unreal and delicate as deer of glass, and he swam in wonder again.

"There's the city already!" Persyvaunce gathered daring enough to point.

A long valley ran down from the mountains, with a river snaking in silver loops down its heart, and in the distance, at its mouth, Ryan could see the hazy sheen of the sea, and beside it, on a promontory, a vague, brownish jumble. Persyvaunce jiggled with excitement, causing Ryan to clutch hard at him.

"There's the king's fortress—" For already they had flown closer, near enough for Ryan to see the gull-gray castle by the waterside. "—and the harbor." Where the masts of tall ships swayed as their sculpted bodies rode on the waves, black against the water and very graceful, very beautiful.

The eagle began to drift downward.

"And the college of wizards!" Persyvaunce declared, pointing. "With the gold-peaked turrets, and the gold tiles."

Ryan caught sight of the building set on a hillside, smaller than the king's castle but very elegant. All through the city he saw spires, towers, gargoyles of carved stone. The city walls rose close at hand, pennons flying from their towers, sun shining off their crown-form summit. And the gates stood ornamented with real gold. The city rose like the kingdom's proud figurehead, aspired to the sky like tall masts, as bright and beautiful as the ships in the harbor.

With a jounce the eagle landed outside the gilded gates. "Here we are!" Persyvaunce cried joyfully, bustling down from their mount, but Ryan sat still, gazing.

"Down, lad, before the creature flies away again."

Persyvaunce pulled him by the arms, and he slid off, stood tottering with the strangeness of ordinary ground. The eagle shook its feathers into place again, clicked the membrane of its eye at him in a sickening way, swooped up into the air without another glance, and wheeled away toward the mountains.

"This way, lad." Persyvaunce tugged at him. "By my bones, you are so weakened from hunger you are reeling."

Indeed Ryan was swaying as he walked, but more from excitement than from hunger as he followed Persyvaunce through the gates that had made way for kings, into the royal city.

Chapter 7

People openly gawked as Ryan walked with Persyvaunce down the narrow streets of the court city, and not in admiration of any grandeur, either. Ryan had never felt so shabby. His clothes had turned to rags from constant wear; his toes stuck grimily out through the tips of his sneakers—outlandish shoes to start with. He badly felt the stares of the townspeople. His face burned, and he fixed his eyes on Persyvaunce's scurrying heels and the cobbles of the street.

"Courage," the little wizard exhorted. Ryan had not seen Persyvaunce slow down or look back, but somehow Persyvaunce knew, as he always seemed to know, what Ryan was feeling. "We are nearly there. In fact, here are the gates."

But Persyvaunce did not go in at the bronzed, filigreed main gates of the college. Instead, he bustled to a side door of that stately edifice. Voices could be heard from the congress hall, but Persyvaunce avoided it. Skirting all the laboratories and classrooms, he led Ryan through a tangle of dim corridor to a spiral stairway, then up it to the top of the tallest tower, to a closed door, where he knocked.

"It had better be important," a deep voice snapped.

"Chin up," Persyvaunce whispered to Ryan. "His bark is worse than his bite."

The door opened, and in the doorway stood a tall, broad-shouldered, gray-bearded man in a sweeping robe of midnight blue. He looked more wizardly than a dozen of Persyvaunce all rolled together. Ryan had to stop himself from taking a step back as the tall man glared at his friend.

"Persy," snapped the other without greeting, "you have the nerve, keeping me up most of the night with your insignificant plaint, and on the eve of the congress, yet!"

Persyvaunce blinked owlishly at this outburst. "I'm sorry, Durnor," he said. "I had no idea my sending worked so well."

"Why should it not work, if you did it the way I taught you? No idea," Durnor mocked. "But you do have an idea, I daresay, now that I've helped you here, that this congress will concern itself with your yellow message of last week. Well, put that idea out of your head. This congress was called on account of a dangerous warlock named Rudd, and it will concern itself solely with him."

"Why, I know Rudd," said Persyvaunce with just a twinkling of a glance toward Ryan. "In fact, I was his bedfellow for part of a night, not long ago."

The effect on Durnor was impressive. The tall wizard stood with his gray beard wagging as his mouth wordlessly opened and closed.

"Might we come in?" Persyvaunce asked gently.

Durnor recovered himself somewhat. "I suppose," he

conceded sourly, and he stood aside to let them enter his high aerie, his skylit tower room, eagle gold and cloud white—or perhaps white as broad-winged migrating swans. As soon as the door had latched behind him, Persyvaunce made formal introductions, in effect beginning the conversation again.

"My lord Durnor, this is Ryan DeWitt, of North—North Carolina, wherever that is. Ryan, this is Durnor, my former master and our grandwizard-by-election. Durnor, my yellow message concerned Ryan."

"So I gathered," grumbled Durnor. "You made yourself abundantly clear last night, Persy." The grandwizard shot out a long arm to yank an ornate bellpull hanging against the feather-sheen brocaded wall. Almost immediately a servant came to the door, and Durnor gave a few curt commands. Ryan's stomach hugged itself and began to howl like a passionate dog. The orders concerned food.

Durnor seated himself, gestured his guests to armchairs, and demanded of Persyvaunce, "Tell me of Rudd as much as you have already told me of Ryan."

"The one concerns the other. A few days after Ryan arrived, Rudd appeared at the cottage, calling himself your envoy."

"Hogwash!" Durnor exploded.

"Of course. Even if you were one to send envoys, he could not have come from you in so brief a time. But he knew of the yellow message somehow."

Persyvaunce continued the tale of Rudd's treacheries. Breakfast arrived. With more wisdom than Ryan would have showed on his own behalf, Durnor had ordered a modest meal of fresh fruit and lightly buttered toast. The servant set it on a small circular table and pulled it close to the visitors, and Ryan could scarcely wait until the man had withdrawn his hands before he lunged at the food. He gobbled while Persyvaunce talked, and noticed too late that he had eaten Persyvaunce's share as well as his own, and stopped, ashamed. But Persyvaunce smiled and offered him the last triangle of toast.

"Go ahead, lad. I'm fat enough."

"Don't be a martyr, Persy. I can order you more." Though he did not in fact order more, Durnor's growl lacked bite, and he seemed to have mellowed considerably since hearing Persyvaunce's story. He eyed Ryan thoughtfully, stroking his gray beard. "Feel better, youngster?"

"Much better, sir. Thank you." It was not true. Ryan's stomach was struggling painfully with the sudden surfeit of food. But no sense in telling Durnor that.

"Are you a wizard in your own world, Ryan?"

The boy felt his jaw drop in his surprise. "Not hardly!"

"I just wondered. There seems to be some sort of link between you and Rudd. Or perhaps I should say, you and your crayon are of some significance to Rudd, because he has taken such a long journey at a crucial time to concern himself with you. But I don't know of what significance." Durnor gave Ryan another searching glance. "You are certain you are not a wizard?"

"We don't have wizards in my world," Ryan answered, adding, "sir."

"I see. What is your world like, then?"

"Very different from this, sir." Ryan struggled to describe how so. "Full of machines."

Durnor said in a low voice, not grumbling this time but quite serious, "I am not at all sure, then, how we wizards are to return you to your own world, as Persyvaunce would have us do. We have no specialists in machines." He turned to the wizard in question. "Well, Persy, it appears your problem will be addressed by the congress after all. Bring young Ryan with you when you come."

"Very good!" Persyvaunce bounced out of his chair and appeared about to caper, then stood still. "Durnor, can the charity of the house provide him with some more proper clothes? He can't go before the congress in those!"

"Of course," said the grandwizard. "And have you thought of asking for some for yourself?"

Looking hard at Durnor, Ryan thought he saw the crinkling hint of a smile. But Persyvaunce seemed not to notice it. The little wizard glanced down at his bedraggled tunic and shrugged.

"Everyone is used to me," he said.

Durnor sternly turned his smile to a scowl. "Get along to your room," he ordered, "and I'll have some sent up. For both of you." He reached up to tug the bellpull again, then looked at Ryan with twilight-colored eyes as unreadable as the yellow ones of the huge birds he had the power to command.

"Do you find our world quite strange, Ryan?"

"Yes, I do, sir. Though I like it."

"You will find our clothing strange as well. Please be

assured it is proper and genteel. Go along, now, and I will see you at the congress." He escorted them to the door and closed it after them.

"That went better than I expected," Persyvaunce whispered to Ryan when the two of them had attained a safe distance. "Ryan, lad, I do believe he rather likes you!"

"He's okay, really," said Ryan. "Isn't he?"

"He's a strong man but a good one."

Already when they reached their room a hearth fire was warming it, and soon a number of servants arrived with a wooden bathtub and pitchers of hot water. Apparently, Durnor had given orders that they should be bathed. ("Though why in the world," Persyvaunce declared cheerfully, "I can't imagine.") Ryan and Persyvaunce soaked in turn, and the hot water soothed the uproar in Ryan's stomach, and afterward, being clean again, he felt more like his own-world self than he had in many days.

The clothing that awaited him, however, brought him back to the wizards' world with a jolt: buskins of tooled wine-red leather, scarlet hose, a long, full-sleeved tunic of creamy linen, a broad leather belt that matched the shoes, and a satin-lined cloak of rich blue broadcloth. The cloak was too short to be of much use against cold or weather and was apparently intended for effect.

"I feel like a sugar-coated prince!" Ryan complained to Persyvaunce. "Is this what people really wear?" He looked with raised brows at the shapeless, raisin-colored robe Durnor had sent up for his friend.

"It's a bit finer than most people wear," Persyvaunce

conceded, admiring him. "But not really royal garb. No broidery, no jewels, but the fit is splendid, the stuff is superb, and all in impeccable good taste. You look magnificent. Durnor must have had a garb specialist magic the things, that they suit you so well. I wonder what our grandwizard has in mind for you."

"Ulp," said Ryan.

"No, no, not at all! Well . . .Well, come along, lad, we had better go down."

The congress hall milled with a motley assortment of chatting wizards: strong youths in important-looking black cloaks, feeble graybeards in pointed hats that looked laughable to Ryan's eyes, and quite a variety of middle-aged men. Boys of about Ryan's age were offering food from trays, their lips parted in excitement or awe.

"Students," Persyvaunce explained. "Can you believe I was ever that young?" And from the shelter of a column he pointed out some of the wizards who had been his classmates. "There's Heneyson. You'll like him; he specializes in horses. And Gye, the one in rose red, works with romantic love, but perhaps you're not ready for that yet. Froll, there, in cerulean blue, he studies the sky. Oh, there's Lionel, a good fellow, deals with food. And Phelot chose poetry. That's not to say he is a poet; he helps poets invoke the muse."

"What is Durnor's specialty?" Ryan asked.

"Birds. Flight is one of the Deep Magics."

"Hallo, Persy!" called several voices as his friends noticed him. Smiling, he led Ryan into the crowd.

"Gentlemen, this is my new and totally unexpected friend and guest, Ryan DeWitt."

Ryan bowed, then listened as Persyvaunce talked to the others. He could tell that they considered the little wizard a bit of a joke, though they liked him well enough. At his first opportunity Ryan turned to the food. He no longer minded the eyes turned curiously on him, and he did not consider it too soon for him to eat again. Hot beef and pork pasties, cheese wedges, apple slices—Ryan devoured enough for three hungry wizards. The food seemed extraordinarily good for such simple fare.

"Lionel has magicked it for our benefit," remarked Persyvaunce, standing beside him and biting into a beef pastie. "I can tell. A good fellow, Lionel."

Ryan grabbed for his fourth pastie just in time. The serving boys all scurried away with their trays when Durnor entered the room.

"Gentlemen, your attention," Durnor rumbled. His voice was not loud, but all chatter immediately ceased as the wizards found seats and faced him. Ryan hurriedly finished his meat pie and did likewise.

"As of this morning, we have a quorum," Durnor informed the gathering. "The congress is now convened."

"As you might guess, our main item of business concerns a warlock. A talented young man by the name of Rudd studied at this house, made his passage last year, but refused the Choice. I will admit to you that I was deeply shocked and shaken. He was one of my personal students, and I spoke for him. I had no inkling he was going to be that kind, none at all."

"I have said it before," boomed Heneyson, "and I will say it again. We ought to employ a mind reader to help us weed out the bad apples."

"That is a mixed metaphor," Phelot retorted sternly. "And this congress has decided many times that a mind reader would make too dangerous a safeguard."

"Just how dangerous," said Durnor, "is to be shown by the fact that Rudd is a superior mind reader himself."

"Why have we not heard of this Rudd before?" Froll demanded.

"My mistake again, colleagues. I thought that the matter would wait until the next yearly congress. Usually it takes some time for a warlock to cause serious trouble. But Rudd is a brilliant and highly self-disciplined young man, and already he has found his niche. He is rapidly rising in the king's favor, and I understand that the two of them are planning a war of conquest. Against Tarq, no less."

All whisperings and stirrings ceased; the room went still as a tomb, with every wizard in it sitting rigid and erect. Ryan could feel their shock hanging like a scream in the air. His hand groped toward Persyvaunce.

"We'll get mangled," the wizard explained to him in an undertone. Because of the deathly silence, Durnor heard.

"Precisely," the grandwizard quietly agreed. "The lion of Tarq sleeps, and dislikes being aroused. Gentlemen, I have mishandled this matter of Rudd, it seems, from the beginning. If you wish, I will resign my post."

A hubbub answered him. "What good would that do?" Heneyson's deep voice sounded above the rest. "Nonsense, Durnor!" cried Persyvaunce. "There's no need for that!"

called Froll. Lionel hitched up his wheat-colored robe and got to his feet.

"All of us together are more than the equal of any warlock," he declared, "as the king would find if he ever had a just war to wage and called on us. We must be united if we are to succeed in this matter of Rudd, not divided by mumblings over any mistakes made in the past, real or imagined. Gentlemen, a vote of confidence for Grandwizard Durnor, if you please."

The vote was unanimous. Durnor stroked his beard to hide his mouth, but he looked, Ryan thought, touched.

"Very well," the grandwizard said gruffly. "I will continue to serve."

"Enough of this foolishness!" bellowed Heneyson. "What are we going to do about Rudd?"

Durnor said, "Concerning Rudd, a peculiar matter has come to my attention that we must take into consideration. You may have noticed we have a visitor in our midst. His name is Ryan DeWitt, and he comes from a world where there are machines but not magic. For reasons I cannot fathom, Rudd has stolen something from him. Persyvaunce, perhaps you would explain. Gentlemen, you all know Aloysius Persyvaunce, our specialist in colors."

The plump little wizard got to his feet amid smiles all around. "It's all my fault," he stammered, flustered. "I was fishing for a nice, agreeable, hearty red, and I got Ryan by mistake, along with a kind of red drawing stick—oh, you needn't laugh!" As amusement rippled around the room.

But all smiles faded as Persyvaunce told the assembly

about Rudd's dealings with him and Ryan. Prolonged discussion followed. No one could understand how Rudd had known of the crayon, or whether he had appeared at the cottage for some other reason, and if so, what that reason might be; and no one could understand why he had stolen the crayon. Durnor introduced Ryan, who stood and was questioned at length about his world in general and crayons in particular, and any magical properties that might be attached to them. He knew of none, except that his red one might help get him back to his own world, if Persyvaunce managed somehow to send it back and send Ryan along with it.

"The crayon is quite beautiful," said Persyvaunce, "and a rarity in our world, and therefore valuable. Perhaps Rudd stole it for no reasons other than those."

Durnor shook his head uncertainly. "Rudd is all intent on magic and power," he said. "Not on rarities. Also, he is proud. Why would he act as a common thief?"

"Nevertheless, a common thief is what he is," grumped Heneyson, "and someone ought to tell the king as much."

Ryan turned to Durnor. "Is that what I should do to get my crayon back? Go to the king?"

"It might be very good for all of us," said Durnor, "if you did. It would discredit Rudd, if the king believed you."

Persyvaunce sensed a drift to the talk that for Ryan's sake he did not like. The rotund wizard stood up in pink-faced alarm, confronting Durnor. "Ryan's concern is with getting back to his own world," he protested, "not with warlocks."

But Ryan had seen the flicker of hope in the grandwizard's

eyes. "I'll help you with Rudd," he offered, "if that's what you mean."

"Durnor," Persyvaunce appealed, but his mentor put him off with a quelling gesture. All the while, Durnor's eagle-keen gaze stayed on Ryan.

"That's exactly what I mean. But I thought it would take much more maneuvering," the grandwizard said. "Why do you wish to help us?"

Under the gaze of those thoughtful eyes, Ryan gave the tall wizard the most honest answer he could. "I guess I've always wanted to be a hero," he said. "Go ahead and laugh."

No one laughed. All the wizards listened in intent silence. "Durnor," said Persyvaunce sharply, no longer to be silenced, "the boy is totally generous. It is not fair to take advantage of him."

"I would not think of it," said Durnor without wrath.

Persyvaunce's round face had settled into a stubborn look. "If the stakes were large enough, you might."

"It is true there is much at stake," said Durnor. "But think, Persyvaunce. It will be Ryan's gain as much as ours if he can get his red talisman back."

"I want to help, Mr. Persyvaunce," said Ryan. "Really."

Persyvaunce lifted his hands in exasperation, then suddenly yielded. Or partially yielded. "Only if I go with you," the little wizard grumped.

Chapter 8

I feel like an idiot," Ryan said to Persyvaunce as the two of them walked down twisting, cobbled streets toward the castle. Though Durnor had assured him he was appropriately dressed for an audience with the king, people were staring at him as much as ever. "Are we going to get thrown in a dungeon?"

Persyvaunce looked startled. "Oh, no, I should hope not!" he cried fervently. "Not if we are respectful. You must call Duald 'Sire.' "

The king's name was Duald. Grandwizard Durnor had briefed Ryan thoroughly on the man. Dagonet, his father, had been a proper hellion. But Duald was in many ways a good king: fair in the court of law, fair in taxation, modest in his spending. He kept only a small garrison. Yet in spite of all such moderation, he was still trying to live up to his father's reputation for glory and thought he could do so by use of magic. He had won some battles by magical means and lost some wars.

"The emperor of Tarq has no such scruples as Duald," Durnor had told Ryan. "He will make mincemeat of us if we annoy him."

"Doesn't Rudd know that?" Ryan had asked.

"He knows it, but he doesn't believe it. He has not yet lived long enough truly to believe in death." The grandwizard had gazed somberly at Ryan. "Yet for some reason you do believe, though you are younger than he, Ryan. Are children of your world reared to think of death?"

Ryan remembered his nightmare vision in the forest and gave no answer.

Durnor's plan was for Ryan to charge Rudd before King Duald with common thievery. Ryan's status as a visitor from another world made him a once-in-a-lifetime rarity among petitioners. It would lend weight to his words and protect him, for the most part, from the king's wrath. If Rudd could be made to lose face before the king, Durnor hoped, if in any way the youth could be made to look like a scheming knave, perhaps the king's infatuation with him would be dampened. Duald was not by nature a shedder of blood. Perhaps he could be made to take pause and think.

"One problem," Persyvaunce had pointed out in his mild way. "We can't say for sure that Rudd took the crayon."

Everyone had stared at him, even Ryan. "Who else would it have been?" Ryan protested.

"Don't misunderstand me, lad. I know it was him, just as well as you do. But we did not actually see him take it."

The assembled wizards had muttered doubtfully. "Durnor," Phelot had protested, "this is madness! To challenge a dangerous warlock with an accusation they cannot prove, you would send a boy and a—er—"

"Incompetent?" Durnor suggested with a smile. "Because he brought Ryan here by accident, you think he cannot deal with Rudd and the king? Ever since I have known him, Persyvaunce has been blundering about; yet things seem always to come to rights for him eventually. Rudd, who is so very clever, should find it difficult to deal with his total lack of guile. And Ryan, also, is guileless."

"So we are to send the innocents to the lions," Phelot had said.

"Wise as serpents and innocent as doves," Durnor had replied with an inscrutable look. "But remember it is Ryan's decision to go, and Persyvaunce's to go with him, not an act of this congress. Though I do suggest that we wait to take action until we see how they have fared."

Then the tall grandwizard had turned to the heroes in question and laid hands on them in a gesture very much like a blessing, sending them off to the castle.

Therefore Ryan and Persyvaunce were making their way down the narrow streets, and through the castle gates with their guardian griffins of carved stone, to the courtyard, and were taking their place in the long line of people waiting to enter the king's audience hall.

Ryan fidgeted, jiggling his legs, feeling the knots in his stomach tighten with every moment. The stones of the castle walls, he noted peevishly, were flannel gray, the same color as his father's business suits. He hated that color. He hated gray citadels and gray metal desks and DeWitt Office Supplies. "I will never understand," he whispered fervently to Persyvaunce, "how I get myself into these things."

"Courage, lad," Persyvaunce murmured. "The waiting's the worst of it."

But the wait was not as long as they feared. The line

moved more quickly than seemed possible, and as the two of them entered the high, arched doorway to the audience hall they saw why. Amid gilt pillars and walls of gold-veined marble and hangings of royal purple, the king sat enthroned on a dais. Beside him, in a carved chair only slightly less ornate than the throne, sat Rudd, lean and handsome as ever in a black robe with sleeves slashed to reveal the crimson silk tunic underneath. Rudd fixed his dark-eyed stare on each person who came before the throne, and almost before the petitioner could plead his case Rudd told King Duald whether the person spoke truth or lies, or whether information had been withheld. With the help of the mind reader, the king was able to settle business at an amazing rate.

"Black seems to be in fashion with the youngsters these days," Persyvaunce murmured to Ryan. "And it is hard to make a good black dye that will not fade to brown."

But Ryan did not reply. He was staring at Duald with a look of startled dismay. "The king!" he whispered to Persyvaunce. "I—I can't talk to him! He looks just like my father!"

"He does?" Persyvaunce regarded the heavyset, balding man on the throne with interest. "How fascinating! But why can't you talk to him?"

"I just can't!" Ryan's eyes had gone wide with panic. "You'll have to do it."

"I'll try, lad. But I always bungle things so. You'd do better."

Their turn for their audience came. Ryan heard his name

announced, found himself facing the king, stepped forward beside Persyvaunce and made his bow, as Persyvaunce did. He tried not to look at Duald, preferring to face Rudd—and Rudd was eyeing him with a cold smile.

At Ryan's side, Persyvaunce sputtered for a moment like a teakettle coming to a boil, then started to stammer out their business. "We—uh—if it please you, Sire—we have come—that is, I have come on behalf of—"

Ryan saw Rudd opening his mouth to speak and shouted out, "No!"

The king stared at him. Everyone was startled into staring at him, even Persyvaunce. Ryan forced himself to meet the king's eyes. "Sire, don't let Rudd speak until we are finished."

Though Duald did not deny the request, or demand, he did not look pleased. "Then finish," he snapped.

"Speak, lad!" Persyvaunce whispered urgently.

So Ryan spoke, though he could not seem to keep a hard edge out of his voice when he looked at this man so much like his own father. "Sire, I am from another world. I got into yours by mistake. When I came, I had something with me, and Mr. Persyvaunce said he thought it might help me get back to my own world. But now it's gone. Somebody took it."

Ryan paused to draw breath and gather nerve, for he was afraid of accusing Rudd. And in the pause, the king turned to his advisor. "Does he speak truth?"

"Yes, indeed, my king." But Rudd was still smiling his cold smile, and Ryan scowled, puzzled.

Duald turned back to Ryan. "What was this thing that was stolen from you?"

"A sort of red drawing stick called a crayon. In my world, it is not valuable at all. But Mr. Persyvaunce says that in this world it is the only one."

"And do you know who has taken it from you?"

"We think we do, sir." In his nervousness, Ryan scowled harder and forgot to call the king Sire. He nodded at Rudd. "Him, sir."

Anger tightened Duald's eyes and whitened the bridge of his nose, though his face scarcely moved. And Ryan knew that angry look, worse than any frown; he knew it so well that he could have wept, and he wanted to step back, afraid, and at the same time, angry himself, he wanted to shout. The king half rose from his throne in his wrath. "Youngster, you forget yourself!" he thundered at Ryan.

But Rudd spoke up softly from his side. "Sire, it's all quite true." And still Rudd smiled.

Persyvaunce and Ryan stood no less astonished than Duald, who sank back into his throne, staring wide-eyed at Rudd.

"You say it's true? You—stole?"

"Yes. But before you condemn me, consider what the youngster is not telling you." Rudd's smile hardened. He stood, tall and impressive in his black robe. "He is a dangerous warlock, young but no less dangerous than an infant viper. The thing I stole from him is his talisman. I took it away before he could use it to do you harm."

And Duald looked down on Ryan coldly, seeing him as his enemy.

The situation felt so familiar that it made Ryan wild with anger. "I'm no warlock!" he shouted at Rudd. "You're the warlock! So powerful, you had to hit me over the head to get what you wanted from me!"

Rudd grinned. "Not I," he mocked. "You ran into a tree. In your terror."

"Thief!" Ryan cried in fury. "Where's my crayon? Where have you put it?" Persyvaunce laid a hand on his arm, trying to calm him. He pulled away.

Rudd's grin broadened, and he slipped his fingers inside his black robe. "Right here," he said, and as if he did not mind showing the crayon to Ryan and everyone else, he pulled it forth.

A gasp rippled around the audience hall. To the farthest corners of the place, all eyes fixed on the small bar of sweet, intensely pure color. Persyvaunce nudged Ryan, directing his glance toward the king. Ryan saw the wonder and longing on Duald's face, and his anger at the man suddenly melted away.

"Rudd," he spoke up suddenly, eagerly, "give it to the king."

Rudd's smile faded as he peered at Ryan. No one spoke.

In his ardor it seemed to Ryan that Rudd must not have understood. "The crayon!" he urged in the same eager tones, though with less ceremony than ever. "Give it to Duald. He wants it. And anyway, Mr. Persyvaunce told me once that kings ought to have crayons like that. He said if they did, maybe they'd make less war."

A deathly silence. Not a person in the crowded room stirred or spoke. Duald stared down on Ryan with whitening nostrils.

"I'll make war whenever I choose," the king finally said, harshly. "Who are you to speak to me of war?"

It was as if his father had said to him, "Who do you think you are?" Furious again, Ryan wanted to turn away and stalk off to his room. But it was not his father speaking; it was a king, and he did not dare move, and he could not think of a thing to say. Persyvaunce sputtered and spoke.

"Sire—uh—if it so please you, it is the concern of all good folk when you think of making war on Tarq."

A gasp and a babble of dismay went up from all the people in the room. King Duald glared first at Persyvaunce, then at Rudd. He had hoped their plans were secret.

"He knows it from old Durnor," Rudd snapped in answer to the look, "and how *he* knows, I can't tell. Footmen, send the people out, all but these two! The king will address no more petitions today."

The retainers hustled the clamoring onlookers out of the audience hall and closed the big doors, leaving Ryan and Persyvaunce before the throne.

"Now." Duald stared at Ryan, looking grim. "What's your game, young warlock?"

"I'm not a warlock!" Ryan exclaimed. "I have no magical powers! Ask Rudd what's his game."

Duald seemed not to hear what Ryan was saying. "Speak truth," he demanded. "What do you want here in my kingdom?"

"I want to go home from it! I want my crayon!" But neither statement came from Ryan with the force of truth. In fact, he did not know what he wanted, of Duald's kingdom or of his life.

Even without the aid of his warlock the king sensed falsehood. Duald said sternly, "You want more than that. You are some sort of spy. Were you sent here by the Tarquin?"

Rudd sat, smiling again, holding the crayon in his hand. And Ryan looked up at Duald with a sudden prickling of tears in his eyes.

"Sire," he said, "we're from different worlds. I don't think like you do. I don't understand you."

"There's nothing to be gained from talking to him, Sire," Rudd said to Duald.

"Go," the king ordered Persyvaunce and Ryan in tones that said: *And don't come back.* They made their bows and left him.

Henry DeWitt shook blood-pressure pills out of a plastic bottle into his clammy palm. "I feel awful," he said to Mr. Chelon. "My chest is tight, and my heart hurts."

Mr. Chelon looked at him closely. "Dreams?"

"An upsetting one, just now, while I was napping. I saw Ryan, and he had that damn stubborn, sullen look on his face, and he was arguing with me. I don't know why he has to be that way! It seems as if we can't talk at all. Either he puts on a stupid look and shuts me out, or, when we do manage to have a discussion, he ends up bolting to his room and slamming the door." Mr. DeWitt got himself a glass of water at the tap and gulped his pills. Then he sat down in the armchair across from Mr. Chelon. A pale, grayish tinge showed on his face, especially along the ridge of his nose.

"What can't you talk about?" Mr. Chelon asked, and Ryan's father flapped his hands in a gesture of despair.

"Just about anything, seems like!"

"But what were you and Ryan arguing about in the dream?"

Mr. DeWitt frowned, trying to remember. Slowly he said, "It seems to me it was something about—about the way I run my business. Ryan is such a dreamer. He has no grasp of what's involved in the business world, the cutthroat competition, the risks, the jockeying for power, the underhanded dealings. . . . Ryan has some terribly naive ideas. That's all very well in a way, but if he's going to run the company after I'm gone, he has to be more realistic."

"Is that what he's going to do?" asked Mr. Chelon.

"Well, yes! I just said so."

"Does he want to?"

Mr. DeWitt stared. "I—I suppose so. I've never asked. My wife and I always just assumed he would. He's our only child."

"Suppose for a moment that there was no DeWitt Office Supplies waiting for him. What do you think he might like to do?"

Henry DeWitt gazed at the small, round man in discomfort and perplexity.

After a long pause Mr. Chelon said, "I think I know

what you must do to help Ryan come back."

Discomfort and perplexity vanished. Eagerly Henry DeWitt leaned forward. "What is it?" he urged. "I'll do whatever you say."

"It is simple, and at the same time very hard. You must make it easier for him to come to you."

Perplexity returned. "How?"

"You must make a change in your thinking. It will come clear to you as we talk."

Ryan's father heard the last word and shouted, "Talk! Not more talk! I thought you said there was something I could *do*!"

"You have always been a man of action, Mr. DeWitt. But magic is more a matter for reflection and the inner powers."

It was the first time Mr. Chelon had spoken of magic.

"This must all seem very strange to you," the little man continued. "Trust me. Please."

"That's the strangest part of it all," said Ryan's father. "I do trust you."

"Well," said Persyvaunce heavily to Ryan as they walked back to report to Durnor, "Rudd's bested us again, lad."

Ryan nodded, though he did not care very much about Rudd. He found himself thinking mostly about Duald. "At least we know where my crayon is," he remarked absently.

"That we do, lad. But the king will never restore it to us."

Duald had been very angry. Ryan recalled the king's

white-bridged nose. Yet Ryan felt more hurt than angry, thinking of him. He wondered briefly, with a pang, if King Duald had high blood pressure, and if the afternoon's shouting had strained his heart.

"I was sending to him the whole time, trying to make him more receptive," Persyvaunce said sadly, "but it seemed not to help at all."

Chapter 9

By the time the congress of wizards convened again, the next day, Durnor had a plan.

"If you'll indulge me for a short while," he told his colleagues, "I would like to propose an act of magic and discuss the point of it afterward. I would like a certain one of you, right here and now, to obtain Ryan another crayon to replace the one Rudd stole from him."

And Durnor turned and looked directly at Persyvaunce.

"By your own methods," Durnor added.

"Oh, no!" The little wizard bounced up, protesting. "No, indeed! You know very well what is going to happen."

Someone behind Ryan stifled a laugh. He looked straight ahead so he would not see the smiles on the watching wizards as Persyvaunce argued with Durnor.

"On the contrary," the grandwizard remarked, straight-faced, "I don't at all know what is going to happen."

"That's what I mean! You know very well I never find what I'm looking for."

"I want you to give us a practical demonstration of your peculiar style of wizardry," said Durnor. "I want these gentlemen to see for themselves the serendipitous nature of your incompetence. Come along, there's a good fellow, I have every faith in you. Up here, now, where we all can see." Durnor moved Persyvaunce's chair to the speaker's platform.

The little wizard still hung back. He challenged Durnor, "What if I bring back another, ah, victim?"

"That will not happen. And I will tell you afterward how I can feel so sure. Come, Persy, no more pretexts."

Sighing, Persyvaunce took the place Durnor had prepared for him. "Gentlemen," Durnor announced to the congress, "a demonstration of magic without reference to the Correspondences of the Seven Spheres."

The room quieted in anticipation. Wishing somehow to show support for his friend, Ryan went and stood near Persyvaunce, on the floor below the platform.

"Crayons," Persyvaunce muttered glumly, mostly to himself. "If I must. A red one, I assume."

"No," Durnor told him, "you've already done red. Try something else."

"Wrong again." Persyvaunce pointedly did not look at Durnor. Instead, he focused on Ryan. "What other colors are there?"

"In the small box? Rainbow colors. Red, orange, yellow, green, blue, violet. Or purple," Ryan added. "I can't remember whether they call it violet or purple."

"Try that," Durnor ordered. "Violet."

"The hardest one! Oh, very well." Persyvaunce spread his hands, closed his eyes, concentrated a moment, then started to chant the words that came to him. "Fileloly aegishjalmur angurgapi achtwan, if it please thee, vy-o-let-te krae-oh-lah—" But before he had finished, a posy of flowers appeared in his hand. The wizards burst into noisy laughter; they could not help themselves. Ryan wished they wouldn't laugh but didn't know what to do about it. He felt angry at Durnor for making a laughingstock of his friend. But Persyvaunce smiled a whimsical smile as he handed the violets to Ryan. "It's all right, you know," he confided. "I really don't mind."

"Try it again, with purple," Durnor directed, unperturbed.

Ryan looked down at the flowers in his hand while Persyvaunce chanted again. He had not known that violets could be buttercup yellow, cream, lavender, and blue as well as purple. They were larger than any he had ever seen, and the largest one was rosy pink. Ryan sighed.

This time, for purple, Persyvaunce received a rustling, translucent, brilliantly purple membrane braced with sticks. Dazzling multicolored strips of gauze streamed from one corner. The wizards did not laugh; they murmured in wonder. "Oh, wow, is that a beauty!" Ryan exclaimed.

"A beautiful *what?*" Persyvaunce pleaded, holding it at arm's length.

"A kite! Don't you have kites here? Take it, Mr. Durnor, it flies."

"It does?" Durnor looked delighted. He actually smiled. "Is it from your world, Ryan?"

"I don't think so." Ryan took the kite and handed it to

Durnor. "In my world, they're mostly made of plastic."

The grandwizard frowned, thinking. "What other colors do the drawing sticks come in, Ryan?"

"In the big box?" He tried to think. Once, years before, he had known them all. "Prussian blue," he said slowly. "Cadet blue, sky blue, powder blue, blue-green, pine green, forest green, spring green, aquamarine—"

"Not blue or green." Durnor's eyes had gone haze-gray, distant. Persyvaunce seemed not to be the only wizard searching.

Ryan said, "Uh . . . Burnt sienna. Bittersweet. Thistle, peach, melon, mulberry—"

"Try mulberry," said Durnor firmly.

The wizards smiled and whispered small jokes to each other, thinking they knew what was going to happen. They expected fruit. But Persyvaunce's spell produced neither mulberries nor a crayon. Instead, there appeared in his outstretched hand a small, shiny, magenta-colored dragon with yellow eyes and spiky turquoise wings. It rattled them over its back and lashed it's serrated tail, glaring at Persyvaunce. The wizard glared back in bug-eyed consternation.

"Take it, Durnor!" he gasped. "It flies!"

But it was Ryan who took the dragon, gingerly, and it settled on his shoulder, preening itself. "From your world?" Durnor inquired.

"No, not hardly."

Durnor considered deeply. "Aquamarine," he told Persyvaunce at last.

"Fileloly aegishjalmur," Persyvaunce started mournfully again. "O sweet lady of uncertainty . . . angurgapi acht-wan, ah-kwa-mah-reen—"

With a plunk there appeared in his hand a silver brooch set with a flashing, sea-green jewel the size of a pigeon's egg. The wizards muttered in awe as Durnor took it and used it to replace the plain clasp holding Ryan's cloak.

"From your world?"

"Maybe. I don't know."

Durnor asked him, "Can you think of a color that might belong *only* to your world? That is like a signature of your world?"

Ryan thought, and felt his mind make one of its crazy leaps, the kind that made him put the wrong answers on fill-in-the-blanks tests. But the answer might be right for this world. "Chrome," he said.

"Chrome?" It was a strange word to Durnor. "Is that a crayon color?"

"Not the last I knew. It's more like a metal. They use it on cars and things."

"On machines?" At Ryan's nod, Durnor told Persyvaunce, "Try it."

"Fi-le-lo-lee-ae-gis-jal-mur-an-gur-ga-pi-acht-wan!" Persyvaunce bellowed wearily. "If it please thee, Bin-nee-Smi-thee-krae-oh-lah kro-mah!"

A bright yellow and green box bearing the numeral sixteen appeared on his palm. Shakily Persyvaunce cradled it in both hands, staring at it as if he hardly dared to touch it.

"Open it!" Ryan exclaimed.

"I—how, lad?"

Ryan showed him. With a trembling hand the rotund specialist in colors pulled up the hinged lid to reveal the glossy, pointed ranks. Each single drawing stick as bright and true as a dream . . . But the pure, shining oxblood red was the sweetest of all. With a glance of defiance at Durnor, Persyvaunce pulled out the red crayon, flourished it as if he had drawn a sword, held it triumphantly over his head. The wizards gasped, then roared. The room vibrated with laughter, cheers, and applause. Persyvaunce popped up from his chair and capered with delight.

"No wonder," said Phelot when the hubbub had somewhat subsided. " 'Chroma' is the old word for all the colors."

"But it's not all the colors!" Ryan objected. "It's nearly the smallest box!"

"This has all been highly elucidating," said Gye, still chuckling. "But what are we supposed to do with the flowers and the crayons and the dragon and the kite and the jewel?"

"All of these items may well be of use," said Durnor, "when Ryan and Persyvaunce go again to confront the king and Rudd."

"Again?" Persyvaunce squeaked.

"Assuredly."

Persyvaunce's yelp—for he considered that he and Ryan had barely avoided the dungeon—his exclamation was overwhelmed in a babble of doubt from all the wizards. Ryan heard a few trenchant voices through the others.

"But Rudd will only make fools of them again!" Gye complained. And Heneyson bellowed, "Are these two the best we can do?"

"Be fair," said Durnor, and the group quieted to listen. "The initial visit was not entirely a failure. Rudd has admitted that he is a thief, and perhaps that will trouble the king. Duald's plan to challenge Tarq has been exposed, and he has not denied it. The news has spread, and the outcry of the populace is urging him to reconsider."

The buzz and murmur of doubt began again. If it had not been for a dragon, a strange flying thing called a kite, a flashing jewel, and a box of crayons, Ryan realized later, the murmur would have been a roar of outright dissent.

Durnor drew himself tall. "Hear me," he said, and though he did not shout, silence followed the words.

"What would you have us do?" he asked the assembled wizards. "All of us together could overpower Rudd, it is true, but then the king would turn against us."

The wizards looked at each other, but no one stood to speak. In fact, no one had a better plan.

"Consider," said Durnor quietly. "Consider that Persyvaunce has been my personal student and I know him well. I tell you, there is more to Persyvaunce than you think. More than he himself knows. Consider Ryan. Why did I feel sure Persyvaunce would bring no other hapless mortal back from Ryan's world? Because I believe Ryan, and Ryan alone, is meant to be here. There is a link between Rudd and Ryan that we do not fully understand. Why did Rudd steal from Ryan? Rudd is clever, but he thinks only of power. Consider this possibility: Can it be that Rudd truly believes Ryan is a warlock? Perhaps Rudd has tried to read Ryan's mind and has seen the outlandish knowledge there. Perhaps he stole from Ryan in an attempt to take Ryan's otherwordly powers to himself."

A babble of talk broke out, more questioning and less doubting than before. Ryan looked at Persyvaunce and rolled his eyes. "I'm no warlock," he said.

"I know it, lad, and so does Durnor." The little wizard looked warily at his mentor. "He's brewing something."

"Let's just say it's so," Gye challenged. "What of it?"

Durnor waited for quiet. The congress of wizards came to attention.

"It means perhaps Rudd will look the fool, and not Ryan and Persyvaunce," said Durnor. "Ryan has a talisman again. It means Ryan can bluff."

Clamor uprose, louder and more vehement than before. Bluffing with a warlock was more than risky; it was foolhardy. "Have you gone mad?" Phelot cried.

"Durnor!" Persyvaunce protested. "Think of the boy."

"Mr. Persyvaunce," said Ryan to his friend, "I've got to do it."

"Lad, it's no joke!"

"I'm not joking. If I can help King Duald, I have to do it, don't you see? He—he's just like my father."

Hearing his voice, the assembly of wizards had grown halfway silent to listen. In the lull, Durnor spoke, very quietly, very seriously, directly to Persyvaunce.

"Old friend," he said, "I am thinking of the boy, more

than you know. I had not wanted to state it so baldly, but—a sense of something fated has niggled at me since I first saw Ryan in those chaotic sendings of yours. You say Ryan's concern is with getting back to his world, not with warlocks, but it is not so. He perceives more truly than you do that Rudd is not a problem he can evade or leave behind. There is a correspondence between the two of them. Rudd is his counterpart in this world."

Utter silence had fallen. All the wizards were listening, and they scarcely seemed to breathe. Ryan looked at Persyvaunce. "What's he mean?" he whispered.

Persyvaunce gave him a thoughtful look. "He means you have a sort of destiny to fulfill, lad," he said slowly. "And though I'd like to keep you out of this if I could, I must admit, no good can come of ducking a destiny."

Durnor scanned the ranks of the wizards. "It is carried, then?" he asked quietly. "There is no dissent?"

There was none. Destiny was a serious business and had to be accepted. Durnor had staked his title, saying what he had said. If he was wrong, he would pay the forfeit. There was no occasion for further argument.

"It is agreed, then," said Durnor. "Ryan and Persyvaunce are to challenge Rudd to a wizard's duel."

"Think back," Mr. Chelon said, "to when you were a boy."

Side by side, Henry DeWitt and his mentor were walking the English countryside. Walking, just aimless walking for the sake of being out and moving, was something Mr.

DeWitt had not done for a long time. The act, the swinging of his arms and the easy pull of his leg muscles, took him back to other things he had not done for a long time. Thoughts he had not thought for a long time. Dreams he had not dreamed for too long.

"What did you like to do?"

"I liked to sing," said Ryan's father. "I sang in the church choir and the school chorus. I sang tenor."

"Did you like poetry, also?"

Mr. DeWitt gave him a surprised look. "Very much," he said after a moment. "At least, some kinds of poetry. Ballads. Poems that told a story."

"And you liked to read."

"I seldom had the chance! There were chores at home for us youngsters to do, lots of work, always. But I liked what we read in school. Plays and such."

"You liked plays?"

"Yes! I acted in some school plays. I was Prince Hal in *Henry IV*. When I went to college, I wanted to—" Mr. DeWitt broke off and stood still, as if listening to some distant song. "I'll be jiggered," he murmured. "I'd forgotten all about that. I wanted to be an actor, but my parents made me major in business instead."

They walked on again. For some time they had been striding up a slow hill. Mr. DeWitt puffed but did not feel he needed his pills.

"They wanted things to be better for us children," he said after awhile. "It was always hard for them. There was never enough money. They didn't want that for us."

Mr. Chelon and Mr. DeWitt reached the crest of the hill and stood scanning the view. Fields and woodlots and stone walls and open meadows stretched away for as far as they could see, like a bright future.

"I don't want things to be hard for Ryan, either," said Mr. DeWitt. "There's a lot to be said for financial security."

Mr. Chelon kept silence.

"But when I think of what I might have been . . . " Henry DeWitt let his voice trail away. "I haven't been to the theater in years," he said very softly after a pause.

"You should start going again," said Mr. Chelon. And absently, still looking at the vista, Mr. DeWitt nodded.

"Which way?" he asked when he had looked enough.

Mr. Chelon met his eyes and smiled.

"It's up to me, is that it? You rascal. You want me to let the boy lead his own life, should I be so lucky as to get him back. Is that what you've been trying to tell me?"

"Please keep in mind that you said it, not I."

"So I did. But it's hard, saying that—that I missed something. That my parents were wrong, or I was wrong to listen to them."

"Perhaps it was not wrong at the time," said Mr. Chelon. "But times change."

"Suppose we just keep walking for a while," said Mr. DeWitt.

They went over the hill and on into the sunlit meadows.

"You look a warlock to give anyone pause," Persyvaunce told Ryan, "with that creature riding like a falcon on your hand." For the bright-colored dragon had settled there during the walk to King Duald's castle.

"And that brooch is stunning," Persyvaunce added. "You understand the plan?"

"Yes. Of course." Durnor had gone over it and over it with them.

Persyvaunce carried the violets. Ryan carried the kite and the dragon and wore the jewel.

"You have the crayon?" asked Persyvaunce anxiously. "Just the red one."

"I have all the stuff," Ryan snapped. Immediately he softened his tone. "Sorry, Mr. Persyvaunce. I just feel like Rudd's going to chew us up and spit us out."

He stood with the little wizard in the castle courtyard, gnawing at his fingers, feeling fear grip his innards as the dragon's dry claws gripped his hand. And though he had mentioned Rudd by name, it was not thoughts of Rudd that frightened him the worst. It was the thought of facing Duald that made him feel weak and sick inside. Most likely the king would roar at them the moment he saw them. It was quite possible he would have them seized and imprisoned for coming before him again. Maybe he would have them beaten. Facing such wrath in an enemy would have been bad enough, but Duald seemed . . . so much like his father, and that made everything—harder. . . .

"For shame," spoke a hoarse, rather scornful voice directly into his ear. "Buck up!"

Ryan jumped as if he had been nudged by a dagger. A pair of vehement yellow eyes met his startled gaze at very close quarters. The dragon had spoken to him!

"You're not alone, you know," it added with a fierce warmth that was, perhaps, typical of dragons.

"Mr. Persyvaunce!" Ryan called, his voice reduced by astonishment to a hoarse whisper. "The dragon talks!"

"Indeed it does," answered the wizard serenely. "And it's quite right, you know. You're not alone."

Chapter 10

"Is this how you heed your king's command?" Rudd shouted. "He bade you go from him!"

"The king did not forbid us to come again into his presence," replied Persyvaunce placidly.

"Let them speak," ordered Duald. "Rudd, sit down."

Glowering, the warlock settled his lean, black-clad body in his ornate chair. And Ryan felt afloat with relief, not because Rudd was silenced but because Duald did not look angry or even annoyed, not for all Rudd's prodding. Instead, the big man looked thoughtful, guarded, almost worried. Something had happened since the last time Ryan had seen him. Perhaps Durnor was right. Perhaps Duald had been thinking about what had been said and wondering about Rudd.

And Persyvaunce seemed much more at ease than he had the day before. In fact, he seemed nearly buoyant with confidence. "Sire," he addressed the king, "if it please you, why do you wish to make war on Tarq?"

Rudd answered instead of the monarch. "The king contemplates war for the expansion of his kingdom and the greater prosperity of his people," he told Persyvaunce.

"For my own fame and glory," said Duald, ignoring Rudd. And though Persyvaunce had asked the question, Duald's gaze fixed on Ryan. "Can you understand that, young stranger?"

Ryan said, "To show your father, you mean, sir?" A sudden feeling of warm affection surprised him and took him a step closer to the monarch.

"*Sire,*" Persyvaunce corrected him.

"'Sir' will do nicely." The king continued to look at Ryan. "When I was your age, my father slapped me across the face if I didn't bow. I detested him, and I could never please him. Yes, I would like to show him."

"But he's dead, sir. And you didn't like him, anyway."

Rudd did not care for what he was hearing, was not pleased by the way Duald gazed at Ryan. "Do not listen to him, my king!" he cried earnestly, laying a hand on Duald's sleeve. "He is a mighty sorcerer! See how already he enthralls you!"

Ryan ignored Rudd and spoke to the king. "War kills people, sir," he said. "Do you like to kill people?"

Before Duald could answer, Rudd rose to his impressive black-robed height again. "Very little bloodshed will be necessary," he declared, "because of my powers."

"Pooh," Persyvaunce spoke up serenely. "You haven't the power of a mouse compared to my friend here."

Duald's gaze on Ryan hardened; the king's eyes narrowed. "You have told me you are no sorcerer!"

"But Rudd says I am," Ryan replied. He looked straight

into Duald's suspicious eyes, willing the king to understand. "Rudd says it was my talisman he took when he stole from me." *Trust me,* Ryan's look requested.

Duald did not entirely understand but leaned back in his throne with a puzzled scowl, waiting to see what would happen next. As for Rudd: He stirred within his black robe like a hawk rousing for the hunt.

"You have experienced my power," he mocked.

"But I am awake now," Ryan retorted with a bold stare.

Rudd's face did not show how taken aback he was, but his hand darted toward the opening of his robe, checking for—yes, the red talisman was still in his possession—

"It doesn't matter, Rudd. I have another one." And Ryan opened his curled fist on which he carried the dragon. In his palm lay a red crayon, a bright, small lance with its tip shining the color of fresh blood, pointed and perfect.

Rudd did not utterly lose his nerve. Scarcely a flicker of fear touched his face. But he seemed to sway a little, setting his long, heavy robes astir as if in a strong wind.

"You can frighten dreamers, Rudd, but you are not capable of answering the simplest questions about Ryan," Persyvaunce prodded before the warlock could recover his poise. "Tell me, for instance: What is the nature of the jewel my friend wears?"

Persyvaunce waited expectantly, looking happy as a good dog. He knew Rudd would find no answers by mind reading. Neither he nor Ryan knew anything of the jewel.

"It's for clairvoyance, of course," Rudd said. "For showing the future, and events far off."

Ryan glanced down. The watery depths of the stone

winked palely back at him. Rudd might well be right. "If it is, the king ought to have it," Ryan said. He took off the brooch, his hands moving awkwardly because of the dragon clinging to one of them and the kite string in the other, but he managed. With the kite over his shoulder, holding the brooch out toward Duald, he stepped up on the dais to present the glimmering jewel in its silver setting. He acted on generous impulse, and just as impulsively Duald's hand reached out to meet his—

"Don't take it, my king!" Rudd shouted. "It is poisoned! One prick of the pin and you will die!"

Ryan gaped at Rudd for only an instant before he jabbed the brooch pin into his own finger so that a small drop of his blood welled up, bright as a red crayon.

Then he offered the gift again, placing it on the arm of the throne beside the king so that Duald need not touch it until he felt sure of it. A shocked silence followed, and not because Ryan had neglected to bow. Duald sat fingering his short beard, knowing that Rudd had been bested.

Persyvaunce pressed his advantage. "Another question, Rudd, of the simplest sort. The dragon you see before you: What is its name?"

The small, bright-colored creature ran up Ryan's arm to lie on his shoulder, its spiny tail encircling his neck. Rudd stood glaring in veiled alarm. Divining names was one of the more elementary magics; yet he could not find the dragon's name in the boy's mind. Truly, Ryan had to be a sorcerer of the most potent sort, to resist him so. Focused on Ryan, he neglected the one mind that could have told him his answer: the dragon's.

"It's Mulberry, of course," it spoke up tartly, its scorn as much for Ryan and Persyvaunce as for Rudd. "And the brooch was to keep the boy's cloak together. Can't you see it's falling off him now? I'm holding it on for him."

"Your tail is jagging me," Ryan told Mulberry in strangled tones. "I can hold my own cloak. Get off."

"Huh!" The dragon gave him a sour look but then scampered down Ryan, like a squirrel down a tree, to the floor, where it poised itself at Rudd's feet. It glared upward with fiery yellow eyes. "Now let *me* ask the mighty warlock a question," it rasped, lifting its spiny wings as if it might attack. "What is the use of a posy of flowers?"

If Rudd had thought of the answer he might have saved himself, for the dragon was a perverse creature, willing to give him a chance. But Rudd did not attempt to divine the answer; he lost his temper. "No more questions," he snapped, his glance, frightened and furious, darting from Ryan to Persyvaunce to the dragon to Duald. "Am I on trial here, that I must answer questions? I will duel any of you, or all of you! I can turn swords into snakes and steeds into tigers; I can frighten armies into rout with my powers. I—"

Persyvaunce looked down at the bouquet of violets in his hand and stroked the large, pink blossom. A bumblebee flew out of it and wove through the air toward Rudd. Once it reached the warlock it started circling his head, leftward, widdershins, the way of magic. Rudd, still ranting, batted at it irritably, scarcely noticing it. His glare turned on Ryan.

"I'll show you!" Rudd cried, lifting his black-gowned arms.

And suddenly Ryan could no longer see the bumblebee, or the king, or the flowers in his friend's hand. He could not see anything but his own nightmare, white fire and blood. Rudd was tampering with his mind.

Awake this time. *Awake,* Ryan told himself grimly, *and not going to let Rudd make a coward of me again.* Something stubborn in him refused to run, not in front of King Duald and Rudd and everyone who was watching. . . . He even kept from screaming, though he bit his lip until it bled. But his trembling legs would not hold him upright. His hand dropped its red talisman to the ground. He groaned and sank to the carpeted dais, his fingers outstretched and feeling for something to cling to. They found only the cold gilt of the throne—

And then he felt warmth. Persyvaunce had hold of him, supporting him, the wizard's plump arms around his shoulders, and everything was bright and real again, and he saw the throne, empty, and the king, taking the two strides that would bring him to Rudd. "Stop it! Stop it, I tell you!" Duald shouted—and Ryan glimpsed Rudd's black, glittering eyes—and then Duald sent Rudd sprawling with a blow of his strong fist.

"My dear boy!" Persyvaunce exlaimed to Ryan. "Are you all right?"

"Now I am."

"It's all my fault! I should have acted sooner."

"You had to wait until Rudd wouldn't notice."

The bumblebee buzzed away from Rudd, heading toward the doors to the courtyard. King Duald reached down, pulled the red crayon out of Rudd's robe, and brought it to Ryan.

"You're no sort of sorcerer at all," he said gently to the boy, "are you?"

"No, sir." With Persyvaunce's help Ryan got shakily to his feet. "I never said I was. Please keep that, sir." He waved away the red crayon the king was offering him and picked up the other one from the floor by his side.

On the throne the dragon was bouncing about, stiff legged and hump backed, like a mongoose. "Rudd!" it mocked. "Ruddy bloody looks-could-kill Rudd! Oh mighty warlock, where is your power now?"

Rudd found his breath in a whoosh of wrath. The warlock sprang to his feet, his face red with fury, and he lifted fiercely hooked hands, shot them at the dragon as if to blast it. But nothing happened except that Mulberry quivered and leaped with dragon laughter. Rudd's face turned ashen.

"My magic!" he squeaked. "They've taken it! How did you do it? Where did you put it?" The squeak rose to a shout, and he glared at Ryan, then lunged. But the dragon flew at Rudd's eyes, and King Duald seized him and pinned his arms behind him.

"You are a thief and a liar," he told Rudd in a voice dangerously low, "and an arrogant twerp, to think you can speak for my mouth. I will now answer Ryan's question for myself. And the answer is this: I do not like killing people. Not even a few."

"Of course not," said a deep voice. Durnor stood at the door, carrying the bumblebee in one cupped hand. As Rudd watched, he gently gathered it in with his fingers, then opened his hand again; his palm lay empty. "I took your magic, Rudd, while Ryan and Persyvaunce distracted you. Surely you didn't think I'd let them face you all by themselves! Ryan and Persy, you've done splendidly."

Durnor stalked in to face the dais, and the whole congress of wizards crowded in after him, their faces stern, somber. King Duald let go of Rudd, and the youthful warlock—or former warlock—made no attempt to move.

"Sire," Durnor addressed the king, "the college of wizards has bestowed on this youngster his powers, and now the congress of wizards has made shift to take them away. It is not something that has been done before, but perhaps it should have been. Much misery might have been saved."

"And the authority of kings would have been lost." Duald stood looking hard at the grandwizard. "Though I know now that my plans were foolish, still I cannot tolerate such interference, Durnor."

"Liege, you need not fear us. We are bound by Choice, and none of us possess warlock power. We must all agree before we can take action such as this, and we are loyal to you." A murmur of agreement rose from the wizards at Durnor's back. "Do you wish to protect Rudd from us? He held your mind in thrall; that is why your plans were foolish. Do you wish us to give him back the powers we have taken away?"

The question hung in the air. Duald looked at Rudd,

and Rudd looked back, and though his face tried to plead, his black eyes glittered hard.

"No," said Duald. "You have done what was necessary, and spared me. . . . Do you wish to punish him?"

Facing the congress of wizards, Rudd did not seem so tall to Ryan anymore, and certainly not dashing. With every breath he seemed to shrink. But the congress of wizards looked to Durnor, and in Durnor's twilight-gray gaze was much the same bleak look as in the eyes of the king. Rudd had been his student and protégé.

"I have small heart for it," he said in a low voice. "Yet I know he has it in him still to make plentiful trouble, though not of a magical sort. Let us together settle on a sentence, Liege."

On the cushion of Duald's throne, the dragon reared, laughing hoarsely, showing Rudd a red mouth and gleaming teeth. "Wow!" it barked at him. "Better run while you can, renegade!"

No guards stood near. Rudd took the taunting advice. He backed away, tossing his head like a shying colt, then ducked behind a tapestry. He had, in effect, exiled himself by fleeing. . . . Therefore the king did not shout for his men-at-arms, and the wizards did not pursue the young fugitive but stood and listened to the fading echo of his footsteps as he hurried away. In a moment they saw him crossing the courtyard. Then he ran out the gates and was gone.

"I feel as if there's a devil lifted off my shoulders," said

Mr. DeWitt to his host. "Words like power, prestige, success, don't hold the whip over me anymore. I've written Emily, but my God, I wish I could speak to my son. I want to tell him how much I've changed."

"Have you dreamed of him today?" Mr. Chelon asked.

"Yes! Quite a lot. He was speaking to me, or with me. We began to understand each other. And then some—somebody, or something, tried to come in the way. I was so angry I jumped up and attacked it. Or him." Mr. DeWitt stopped speaking, looking puzzled.

"Which was it," asked Mr. Chelon dryly, "an it, or a him?"

Henry DeWitt did not answer at once. When, after a while, he spoke, his words came slowly. "It was—I don't know how to explain. . . . It was the son I had made for myself, in my mind. Not the real one, but a false thing. The lies I told myself."

Mr. Chelon suggested, "Call it the devil, whispering in your ear. And he's likely to be back, you know."

"You think so?" Mr DeWitt looked at him in alarm.

"Do not worry. Be proud that you sent him away. You will send him away more easily each time."

Mr. DeWitt nodded.

"You may return to your wife now," added Mr. Chelon, and Henry DeWitt jumped up and exclaimed at him in consternation.

"Without Ryan? My son, man! Where is my son?"

"Unless I am very much mistaken," said Mr. Chelon, "he will be back shortly. He is longing for you, and my counterpart and his colleagues will do their utmost to help him, and I may do a little meddling as well. The sending works both ways, you know." Mr. Chelon looked hard at Ryan's father, who was standing with his mouth working in an uncertain way. "No, you don't know? But you've been doing it yourself. . . . Well, never mind that. Ryan will return soon, to Magic Island, and you will want to be there to meet him."

Mr. DeWitt seemed scarcely able to speak. "Thank you," he whispered finally. "I—is it really going to be over? I can scarcely believe—I don't know how to thank you enough. Anything I can ever do—"

"Never mind all that," said Mr. Chelon gently.

"I'd better book a flight at once!" Still bewildered, Mr. DeWitt looked around anxiously for a phone, though he knew there was none.

"No need," said Mr. Chelon. "I'll magic you back."

Speechless again, Mr. DeWitt gawked at him. Mr. Chelon smiled.

"I am far more efficient than my counterpart," he assured the big man. "I have benefited from the lessons of science." He got up to stand with Henry DeWitt. "Let me shake your hand now. There's no need to pack your bags; it will all take care of itself. I am going to magic you back to the day your son disappeared. It would be a shame if the three of you missed your vacation."

Ryan's father swallowed, accepting all of this much more easily than he would have a few weeks before. He shook Mr. Chelon's hand. "Will I remember you?" he asked.

"Of course, my dear fellow, of course you will!" Mr. Chelon's face grew more than ever pink. "And I will think often of you and send you dreams from time to time."

"I loved and trusted him as a son," said Duald in a low voice, looking after Rudd.

All the wizards glanced down at their hands. Ryan looked down also and knew he wanted to give the king something. Already Duald had the brooch and the red crayon. The violets lay scattered and wilting on the floor. The dragon had leaped to Duald from the throne and rode on the king's shoulder. Wordlessly Ryan approached and offered the glistening purple kite.

Duald's fingers closed numbly around it. But then he looked at the boy and his eyes grew keen. "What is this?" he asked.

"A kite, sir. A sort of flying thing magicked out of another world. But there's no magic to flying it, sir," Ryan added.

"There's not?" Durnor exclaimed, speaking out of turn. Ryan continued to look at the king.

"I'll show you," he offered. "Can we go up to the—whatchacallit, the top of the castle?"

Duald looked at him a moment longer, his eyes thoughtful. Then, as if he had decided something, he handed the kite back to Ryan and with grave courtesy led the way to the battlements. Everyone followed.

A stiff, steady breeze blew off the sea, scouring the platform. Ryan's cloak flapped; he slipped it off and let it lie. The kite threatened to tear in his grasp. King Duald faced the wind like an eagle, the dragon alert on his shoulder. All the wizards stood in a cluster, waiting.

"This way," Ryan called to turn the king around, and he lofted the kite. He sent it up gracefully, gently. Light streamed with crystalline brilliance through tissue of porphyry hue, whelk purple, the color of royalty.

"Lovely!" Durnor breathed, forgetting himself again; the king should have spoken first. But Duald seemed not to hear. His eyes on the sunlit flying thing, on its bright streamers rippling in the breeze, he murmured, "I have never seen anything so beautiful."

"Here, sir, would you like to hold it?" Ryan handed him the string. "Let it out a little at a time." He went and stood with Persyvaunce.

In the courtyard, far below, a crowd of curious people gathered to watch the graceful purple thing fluttering and dipping and rising ever higher above the battlements. From time to time an even brighter shape would fly up and circle the kite. Then the dragon would return to Duald's shoulder. All the work in the castle stopped; the servants came out to watch, and in the town streets the shopkeepers stood in front of their doors, gaping. Housewives put away their mops and came out into the light.

By sunset, the kite had climbed so high that it was no more than a dark spark amid a sky full of orange and indigo glow. "It will take awhile to bring it back in," Ryan told the king. "Do you want me to do it?"

"I think I would rather just let it go," Duald said. "It tugs so. Do you mind?"

"No, of course not. It's yours. Let it go if you like."

King Duald opened his hand, and the kite flew away into the twilight over the mountains. Duald stood watching it go long after it could be seen, and the wizards turned and tiptoed away. But Ryan stayed with the king, though every time he looked at the monarch he felt a lump in his throat.

For the first time since he had come to this wonderful, colorful, magical world . . . just that day, as he had talked with Duald and met the king's eyes and he and the big man had started to understand one another . . . just that day, Ryan had begun to miss his own father terribly.

Chapter 11

Ryan did not return to the college of wizards until long after dark. Then there were questions to be answered, talk and dinner and more talk. Finally, very late that night, he found himself seated with Persyvaunce and Durnor in the grandwizard's tower room. The three of them were nibbling a bedtime snack of milk and cherry muffins, gooseberry jam, wheat bread, raspberries, yellow cheese, elderberry wine, and crumpets. Ryan ate only a few crumpets.

"You're not doing your share, lad," Durnor chided. "Aren't you hungry after such a long day?"

"Lot on my mind," Ryan muttered.

A small silence. "So the dragon stayed with the king," Durnor tried again after a short while.

"Yes." Ryan roused enough to smile. "Mulberry must have liked sitting on the throne."

The little dragon had perched on the king's knee as soon as Duald had seated himself and had spent the rest of the day there or riding on his shoulder. And Ryan had noticed a smile, once or twice, as if Duald appreciated the honor the proud, bright-winged creature bestowed on him by its presence.

"But you haven't kept anything for yourself, youngster," Durnor teased. "Duald has the brooch, the dragon, your crayon, and I daresay the flowers!"

Ryan shrugged, lying far back in his armchair. "He asked me to stay and be his son," he answered in a low voice.

Both Durnor and Persyvaunce stared. "And what did you reply?" the grandwizard asked quietly after a moment.

"I told him I wished I could. And that's the truth, and I hope he could see it. I like him." Ryan swallowed.

"But?" Durnor prodded.

"But I have to find a way back to my real father. I want to be with my own parents again!" Ryan burst out suddenly, tears in his voice. His eyes stung, his heart ached for the fussy, annoying, commonplace couple named DeWitt.

"Of course, lad," said Persyvaunce gently.

"But, Ryan," said Durnor just as gently, "what if we can't get you back?"

"You've got to!" Ryan sat up straight in near panic.

"Durnor, don't upset the boy!" Persyvaunce protested.

"I don't mean to, Persy! But I won't lie to him, either. We don't really know how to send him back."

"I'll send him back right enough if I can find the rule of colors!"

"Persy, I doubt if you will ever be able to find *any* rule," Durnor said, though not at all harshly.

"But of course I expect all our colleagues to help!"

"We will try our utmost. But, Ryan, if we can't—though

you know I hope we can—but if we can't, why, you could be a prince."

Ryan looked down at his hands and thought briefly of princely adventures and glory, a splendid, fiery-red horse, tall ships sailing. He shook his head, blinking.

"I want to go home," he said, not quite able to keep his voice from trembling. "But if I can't, I'll go back with Mr. Persyvaunce. That's my home here."

"My dear boy," said Persyvaunce huskily, "I'll never forget that, whatever happens. And I have my crayons, too, to remember you by. Such bliss."

Ryan had almost forgotten about the crayons. "Only sixteen!" he complained, trying to change and lighten the subject. "I can't understand why in the world they didn't send you the big box of all the colors."

"My dear boy, sixteen is quite enough! More than I had ever dreamed of!"

"I should think so," growled Durnor. "Ryan, boy, get to bed. You look done in."

He found his way to his room and stumbled into his bed, dazed and exhausted after the events of the day. But he did not sleep very well. The goose-down mattress was too soft, and he kept dreaming vivid dreams of yearning kings and bright-colored dragons and kite-shaped flying vellums. The dragons flew far faster than the vellums; in fact, they flew circles around them. Wheeling, spinning, whirling circles as round as the emblems of the wizards, red, orange, yellow, green. . . . The rainbow dragons flew into a blur of blending color that reminded Ryan of something he had once seen, years ago, in another world, in a classroom where he wasn't listening. . . .

The next morning, after a modest breakfast of eggs, fried potatoes, and kidneys, Ryan told Persyvaunce, "I think you did sort of get all the colors in that box, after all. I had a dream about it."

"Quite all right, my dear boy, quite all right, whether I did or not." Persyvaunce felt expansive after yet another good meal.

"No, I think you did, really. Let me see."

He took the yellow and green box from Persyvaunce, pushed back his greasy plate, and tried to lay out the crayons in some sort of order or pattern. Vaguely he remembered a dream and a spinning, circle, circle. . . . He started with white and pink and red, because he knew that pink consisted of white plus red. But red also was in orange, and in purple, and he didn't know what to do with brown or black. Brown was a mix of many other colors, a tree-trunk color. . . . In a minute he laid aside black and white, brown and pink, and started again with yellow, the lightest remaining color. Yellow, yellow-orange, orange, red-orange, red, red-violet. . . . It was easier than he had thought. He let the printed names guide him.

Some wizards had gathered around. "What are you doing?" Durnor asked, his voice loud with excitement.

"Wait," Ryan breathed. "Just wait and see." The last crayon was yellow-green. He placed it in the remaining space, next to yellow. Twelve crayons lay on the table like the spokes of a wheel, with the lightest color, yellow, at the top, and the darkest one, purple, at the bottom.

"A magic circle!" Persyvaunce exclaimed in utter delight. "A color circle! Look, it is like a rainbow bent end to end. Or rather—a harmony . . ." The little wizard made windmill gestures, unable to describe how the circling colors seemed to melt into each other.

"All the colors in the world are in there," Ryan said. "I think brown and all those other colors in the big box are just mixes of these ones and black and white. That's why I say you got all the colors, Mr. Persyvaunce."

Eager chatter began as the wizards argued the point. Heneyson's voice, as usual, rose above the rest. "Some of those are combinations of the others!"

Ryan removed all the crayons with colors that could be mixed from other colors, until only three were left that could not: yellow, red, and blue. "I think those are called primaries," he said.

"Primaries are the large feathers on the wings of a bird," said Durnor.

"Primaries are the spheres around which other spheres revolve," said Froll.

"Primaries are the old words from which all other words began," said Phelot.

"Lad, this is a Deep Magic, what you have done here," Persyvaunce told Ryan with widened eyes. "How did you hit upon it?"

Ryan answered, "A teacher showed me something like this once. If you color a circle in wedges of these colors, the way I have them laid out, and if you spin it very fast, you see a sort of a shine, like chrome."

"The color of all the colors!" Persyvaunce gasped, bouncing up from his seat by Ryan's side. "Ryan, we must do it!" All the wizards burst into excited talk, and Durnor voiced their thought.

"Ryan, you may have found the rule of colors," he said. "And if so, you may have found the way back to your own world."

Ryan's heart started pounding, and he leaped up with such force that he overturned his chair. "Do you have some thin white cardboard?" he demanded.

They did not. Paper was not known to them. The crayon box, made in outlandish design of a bright-colored, mysterious material, seemed to them nearly as much of a wonder as the crayons themselves. For Ryan's project, they stiffened some fine white linen with a thin glue made of bits of boiled parchment. They bonded three layers together, stretched them on a waxed board, tacked them down, coated them with fine gesso, and left them to dry. The drying would take at least a day, though Durnor ordered servants to stand by and fan the air to speed the process, for Ryan could barely sit still.

In the afternoon, news came that stopped his pacing for a few moments. A servant burst into the hall where the wizards congregated. "Have you heard!" the fellow gasped, wide-eyed.

"Heard what?" Durnor snapped. "It had better be important!"

"The dragon! The little one you call Mulberry. It's no dragon at all!" The servant paused for effect.

"Oh, dear," Persyvaunce murmured, at once fearing trouble. The other wizards leaned forward to hear, and Durnor roared at the servant impatiently.

"Well, what, then!"

"A lady! A perfectly beautiful lady!" The man stood relishing his moment of glory as the bearer of startling news. "An ensorcelled princess, she says she is, and only a true and righteous king could free her from the spell. And she declares she will marry him!"

"Good," said Ryan. "Duald has someone to be with him, after all." He spoke quietly, more to himself than to anyone else, but all eyes turned to him.

"Go see him, lad," Durnor suggested.

Ryan did. Princess Mulberry—or Rosemary, as she was more properly named—met him at the door to the king's private chamber, and he would have known without anyone's telling him that she came from another world. Her face had an eerily sculpted look to it, like a ship's prow, set with topaz eyes. She wore a dark magenta gown and a silk capelet, a flash of turquoise. The color of her hair, amber, matched her eyes, and though she seemed not to know how to smile, her eyes smiled, quizzical, feisty, ardent.

"Ryan, lad!" Duald spoke over her shoulder. "Come in and sit down."

He sat on the thickly carpeted floor, where he felt most comfortable, facing the king and his betrothed.

"I am glad to see you, Ryan," the lady said in a low, throaty voice. "I've wanted to thank you for trusting me as you did and taking me to the king. You are very brave, you know."

"Not really," Ryan muttered. He did not feel brave. In fact, he was starting to feel more and more frightened, though not of anything in the wizards' world.

"Brave and good-hearted," the lady insisted. "I felt sorry to leave you. But I needed a king's kiss to break the spell."

That startled Ryan into looking up from the floor. "He *kissed* you? While you were still a dragon, I mean?"

Duald smiled, unperturbed.

"Just a peck on the head," Mulberry assured Ryan. "It was enough." She turned gratefully to Duald. "But it had to be the kiss of a true king."

"I guess you told him what to do," Ryan said.

"No, no! I couldn't. He had to do it on his own."

Ryan's jaw dropped. "But how did he know to do it?"

Duald said, "How did you know what to do, Ryan, to make me see you truly? When you jabbed that brooch pin into your finger, how did you know it wasn't poisoned?"

Ryan gazed back at him without speaking.

"You didn't know," said Duald. "Exactly. We take certain risks." Somehow the king's hand had found its way into the maiden's. "It's really—really extraordinary, Ryan, what you have done for me."

Ryan swallowed and, because he did not know what to say, blurted out the truth. "I've come to tell you good-bye," he told the king, "in case I don't see you again. The wizards are going to try to send me back to my own world tomorrow."

Duald's face turned very still. "I'm glad for your sake," he said after a moment, "but I'm sorry for mine. Ryan, if it doesn't work, my offer still stands, to take you as my son and heir."

Every time Duald said that, Ryan ached more strongly for his own father and mother, his own family. "Please stop," he said, and he got up. "I'd better go." Then, seeing the look on Duald's face, he went back to the monarch and hastily hugged him—surprising the king, but not displeasing him—before he hurried out, running back to the college of wizards.

That night he could not sleep at all. He paced the corridors of the college, going down to the first floor, where the meeting hall and the laboratories stood dark and empty, so that the sound of his footsteps would not disturb anyone. And some time after he was certain everyone else in the place was deeply asleep, someone moved in the shadows beyond his pool of candlelight, and Rudd stood before him.

The two of them stood and stared at each other for a moment. Ryan had been so intent on his own thoughts that he could not feel really afraid, even though he knew no one would hear him if he called for help, even though it took him a moment to remember that Rudd had lost his powers and could not hurt him any longer except by ordinary means, a blow of his fist, a knife . . . did Rudd want to hurt him?

"What do you want?" he asked levelly. It occurred to him how reckless Rudd was to be there. Ryan had heard the decrees; the former warlock risked imprisonment by being in the court city. Mad for revenge, perhaps?

"I want to understand," said Rudd with something odd in his voice. "Who or what are you?"

"I'm just Ryan."

"What do you mean? You summoned me to that wretched besplattered pigsty of a cottage. I could scarcely stop even to sleep; I was pulled there as if in an unseen net of will. And you tell me you are no sorcerer, and then you call me liar!"

Ryan's mouth dropped open, for with sudden insight he understood what had happened. "Persyvaunce summoned you!" he exclaimed, and he began softly to laugh, though not at Rudd. "He was casting about for a strong red, and your name is Rudd, and that means 'ruddy' or 'red' or something like that, doesn't it? Don't you see? It was all a stupid—" Laughter choked him so that he could not speak.

"A mistake?" Rudd stood for a moment with a listening look, then firmly shook his head. "I cannot believe that. I am drawn to you still. I am here again tonight."

Ryan stopped laughing, for now he recognized the odd catch in Rudd's voice: a hidden heartache, a slantwise sort of longing. He knew that longing from his early days at Persyvaunce's cottage, when he had longed for his parents and smothered the ache under anger. He said quietly, "Persyvaunce sent for both of us at once, is what happened. Durnor said he believed you and I were linked somehow. He called it a correspondence."

Rudd said with a hint of his customary arrogance, "Durnor loves to make such pronouncements. But this time he may be right."

"But we're so different. And you are older."

"We need not be entirely alike." A lecturing tone slipped into Rudd's voice. "There are greater and lesser degrees of correspondence between the worlds and the people in them. Your world is very different from ours. Most people in either of those two worlds would have no counterpart at all in the other. It is natural that we should be rather different from each other."

"But I told you the truth," Ryan insisted, "when I said I have no magical powers."

"You may have been telling the truth as you perceived it. And for the matter of magic, I have no powers either, any longer."

Ryan stepped back, for suddenly he felt afraid of Rudd again. "I'm sorry," he muttered. "I keep forgetting."

"I do not like what is happening," said Rudd in a low, bitter voice. "I feel myself growing more like you. Already I have become too chickenhearted to avenge myself on you as I ought."

"No wonder I was beginning to like you a bit better." And Ryan felt an uncanny, silent explosion of joy, because for the first time in his life he knew he liked himself. But at the same time he understood how Rudd felt. He understood because he could put himself in Rudd's place. And in a wordless way he knew what his great gift was, a gift that to Rudd seemed almost magical: imagination. The power to take mental leaps, to make connections.

He said to Rudd, looking straight into the black-clad youth's eyes, "I think I am getting to be more like you, too." For there was no denying that Rudd, though misguided, had been clever and bold. Ryan stood tall. Perhaps someday he would be as tall as Rudd. He said, "Tomorrow, if things work out all right, I'm going back to my own world. If you want to try to hurt me, this might be your last chance."

Rudd stared. His fists curled at his sides as if he wanted to give Ryan a beating, but he did not move. And in a taut voice the tall youth said, "Not here. Not now. But I will fight you, count on it. You will struggle with me every day of your life if I have my way."

Rudd turned and strode away into the shadows.

"Huh," Ryan said to himself. "You won't have your way." He felt suddenly quiet and calm inside, and sure of himself. He went back to his room and slept the few hours that remained in the night.

The next morning the wizards carefully scribed and cut a circle from their linen board, marking off twelve wedge-shaped sections. The actual coloring was to be done by Ryan and Persyvaunce, by a common consent that scarcely needed to be spoken. Ryan started the work, to show Persyvaunce how it was done, and the little wizard groaned as the linen marred the perfect tips of his crayons. But he soon fell in love with the process of coloring itself. The crayon took well to the scratchy surface. Heads nearly touching, Ryan and Persyvaunce colored slowly and carefully.

Ryan found that his hands were sweating. All his calm had left him, and the confrontation with Rudd the night before seemed like a dream. He felt shaky inside. "I'm scared," he said softly.

Persyvaunce paused with his crayon lifted, looking at Ryan. "Of what?" he asked.

"Of going back. My parents."

"You're afraid of your own parents?"

"You don't understand. Everything's different here. What if I go back there and everything's just the same? Sometimes I think they don't even like me. They're always pushing at me. I wish I could stay with you." Ryan felt his eyes fill with tears.

Persyvaunce laid down his crayon and put his arms around the boy. Ryan let his head rest against the wizard's shoulder.

"My dear friend, I wish, too, you could stay." Persyvaunce spoke with emotion thickening his voice. "But you know your heart won't let you. Now, let me ask you something." Persyvaunce's hands gently urged him erect, so that their eyes met. "Why would the brave young stranger who faced and outwitted a most fearsome warlock, and who argued his way into the heart of a king—"

"Cut that out," Ryan said, smiling in spite of himself.

"What I mean to say, my dear boy, is that the lad who faced Rudd has no business being afraid of anything. And can your father and mother be more fearsome to talk to than a king?"

Ryan turned back to his task, picked up his crayon, and colored for some time in silence. Then he said to the linen circle, "I guess I am going to have to do more talking to them and less walking off to my room."

"Indeed," said Persyvaunce.

"I am going to have to say what I think."

"Excellent," said Persyvaunce.

"Maybe I can change things."

"You certainly did here."

"Thanks," Ryan told him.

"Not at all."

"No, I mean . . . thanks for everything."

"Not at all," said the little wizard.

The rainbow-colored circle shimmered, they had crayoned it so long and so well. It was finished. They took it out to where the wizards waited, and a murmur went up. Even Durnor was impressed.

"We shall present it to the royal museum," he declared. "What now, Ryan? Will you stay and eat a last meal with us?"

"No. Thank you, Mr. Durnor, but let's just get on with it." Ryan felt too strained to stay much longer. He helped tack the color circle to a rod, lightly, through the exact center. All the wizards stood gathered around. "See if it will spin," Ryan said.

Durnor made the circle spin. The kaleidoscopic colors flashed together into a brownish pool, then a lighter, brighter shine—what was the name of the color all colors made? Ryan couldn't remember; he felt weak and sick. Arms encircled him, supporting him.

"I hadn't expected it to work so fast," Persyvaunce murmured. "Good-bye, dear boy. . . ." The wizard kissed him, then cried, "Now, Durnor, spin it hard! Everybody help!" Ryan heard the beginning of a chant and felt himself wheeling into oblivion.

Chapter 12

Ryan found himself standing outside Magic Island's general store on a sun-yellow day. A small box of crayons lay by his feet. He picked it up and looked; the red was not there. Ryan smiled with relief. His parents had not had a chance to miss him, after all. They had not suffered, and there would not be too much explaining to do. He started to put the crayons in his jeans pocket—

No jeans, no pocket! There he stood in the dusty main street of a small North Carolina town in an embroidered saffron tunic, royal blue hose, a wide, red leather belt, and pointed boots. Already people were craning out of doorways to gawk at him. Ryan turned and fled toward the sand dunes and the rented cottage.

And as he rounded the last dune his parents ran to meet him, tears on their faces, and then they were both hugging him at once, hard enough to take his breath away, and he did not mind that he was crying, too.

"You've grown," Mr. DeWitt told him huskily.

He pulled back far enough to look into his father's face.

"You look younger," he said. "What's happened? I was afraid—I thought your blood pressure would be up and everything."

"No! I'm much better. A lot has changed. I have some explaining to do."

But Ryan knew that somehow everything was understood, that he himself would not have to explain much to them or anyone else, and he felt his life lift into place like a sail into sunrise.

A day later, after an afternoon and evening of eager talk, a long night's sleep, and a festive breakfast, Ryan found a use for his seven remaining crayons.

"Mom, do we have a ball of string?" he asked. "I'm going to try to make a kite."

He had told something about Duald and the kite and how beautiful it had been. His mother looked at her son where he stood luxuriating in the good feel of his oldest jeans. "Why, I'm sure we can find some somewhere. Ryan, what a lovely idea," she said softly. "May I help?"

They all helped. They cut the kite out of a white paper bag, colored it with crayons, and pressed the bright designs into the paper with a warm iron so they would shimmer in the light. Ryan and his father made a framework out of slats from the roll-down window blinds. Mrs. DeWitt brought a ball of crocheting cotton ("Pearlescent Mauve, Medium") by way of string, and a feather-light head scarf for a tail.

They all took the kite out to the dunes, and it flew at

once in the steady sea breeze, buoyed up as if by magic. Ryan let his parents fly it most of the time. He sat and studied the sea. It reminded him of the blue smalt glass Persyvaunce had sometimes ground for pigment. The dune grasses stood porcelain green against sand that sparkled with bits of pink and terra-cotta shell. Ryan marveled at all the colors he had never noticed; why had he not seen them before? And behind him his parents laughed, running and playing like young kids.